How to Leave a Place

26 Short Memoirs by Portland Writers

How to Leave a Place

26 Short Memoirs by Portland Writers

Edited by Ariel Gore

Contents

The Language of Your Life

WE ARE A COMMUNITY of writers who gather at The Attic on Hawthorne Boulevard in Portland, Oregon. We are doctors, waitresses, housewives, and punks. We are grandmothers, rock stars, and runaways. We are sixteen or sixty-seven. We're from Brazil; we've just moved to India. We grew up in San Francisco, Dublin, Quito. We're third generation Northwesterners or we've only just arrived. We complain about the rain, but we don't seem to mind it that much. We drink a lot of coffee and beer. We make zines, collages, music, sugar cookies. We've been telling stories, in one way or another, for as long as we can remember. We expand our writing skills by receiving and giving feedback. Collectively, we are brilliant. We explore our own life stories, become engrossed in each other's. We follow the sentence to the end, always wondering what will come next. We write, rewrite, edit, and occasionally just start over. Sometimes we ignore the facts to tell the truth. Or we change names to protect the guilty. We bank on chance, and skate on by. We read at STS and Dexter's open mic on the northeast side of town. We drink wine to gain courage; smoke with satisfaction when the story's been read. We are a community of writers who gather at the Attic on Hawthorne Boulevard in Portland, Oregon. And we want to tell you a story. Thanks for listening.

—Twenty Portland Writers

WHERE I'M FROM

Leaving Compton

Ann Rogers-Williams

MY BIRTHDAY IS COMING and I'll be five years old. But right now the whole house is full of boxes and furniture pushed into the living room. My Mum and Dad are busy all the time and cranky most of the time. Someday soon we will be moving, Mummy tells me.

They look like they need some help so I start moving my furniture, too, as best I can, into the hallway. I can lift my little chair and my laundry basket of toys. It feels good to be like the grown ups. Daddy sees me and I am proud to show him how I can help. But he yells at me, so I go outside to help the ants move their furniture instead.

I find them busy, working on a new project, building a new home in the big dusty spot in the lawn. I look up and see Didi coming! Didi is my friend from next door. She's the same age as I am, but she's a little smaller. We play outside together all the time. I call to her, "Hey, Didi, you wanna watch the ants with me?"

The ants are the only animals I have left since my turtle died. My mother forgot about him and left him in a box in the sun. That was after she gave away all the kittens plus the mama cat. Daddy thinks animals are messy.

Didi thinks ants are boring, so I say, "OK, wanna draw then?" Didi doesn't have any crayons or drawing paper, her parents don't buy that kind of stuff. I tell her she can use mine. I've got crayons. I've got lots of crayons. But she gets mad at me for saying that. I don't understand why she's so mad, so I get mad at her.

We get mad about dumb things sometimes, and then we both run home until it's after nap or sometimes until the next day. Then we come back to meet at the dusty spot in the grass between our houses and I say, "I'm sorry, Didi." And Didi says, "I'm sorry, too, Boo." And then we start playing again like always. It's not a good habit, we know. We just like the sound of our words. Like when I walk around saying "nevertheless," and Didi walks around saying, "ridiculous" just like the people on TV.

But this time we get in a fight over stupid crayons and I get mad and yell, "Didi, I hope I never ever see you again."

Didi stops breathing and looks at me. Then she says, "Well, fine by me. I hope I never ever, never, ever see you again, too."

"Fine by me!" I say.

And Didi says, "Fine."

We look at each other for a second, and then we both run home.

The next morning, I'm waiting for Didi. There's lots of stuff going on in my house, and I hope she will come out soon. Mum says I must stay put and not go running off anywhere. So I just look in Didi's back yard to see if I can see her. But her yard is quiet.

Some Bekins men came early this morning and they are loading up a truck with our boxes and it looks like maybe we really are moving soon. I keep looking and waiting for Didi. The stuff in my room is all packed up now, and the Bekins men are carrying away the furniture. You know, I think we may be moving *today!*

Maybe she's sick. Or maybe she's getting new shoes. I want to run out to the street and knock on Didi's front door. But I'm not allowed to leave my yard. I look across at her window on our side, but I don't see her. Her house is quiet.

Now the boxes in the kitchen are disappearing into the truck one by one. Mum and Dad are busy loading boxes into the car. They don't have time to say much to me.

I want to tell Didi I'm sorry. I want to tell her it's OK that she doesn't care for ants or have any crayons.

It's almost lunchtime, but we have no table or dishes or anything. Mum gives me a sandwich to eat on a paper napkin. She says I can eat it outside. So I go back outside and sit on the steps for a minute. I go over to the dusty spot where the ants live and leave my sandwich there. *I'm so sorry, Didi.*

The men and the Bekins truck are gone now. Mum and Daddy have finished loading up all the boxes into the car. They put me in the car last. And we drive away from Compton forever.

☼ Sinners

Linda Fielder

MOTHER INFORMED ME one morning that I'd be starting first grade on Monday at a nice Christian school. My family wasn't religious, but talk of bussing in our Indiana town had prompted my mother to find a school that was close to our house, required an outrageous tuition, and listed God as its superintendent. Her problems were solved.

I looked forward to my first day at the Christian school. I liked what I knew about God from my annual Easter visits to Sunday school. Last Easter I constructed an intricate felt and macaroni cross, and I planned to take it with me on my first day of school to impress the teacher. I was feeling very Christian for a six-year-old.

The teacher, Mrs. Green, seemed genuinely moved when I presented the macaroni cross, but by the end of my first week it had become glaringly obvious that I didn't fit in. My parents weren't deacons or missionaries, my hair wasn't long like the other girls, I didn't have a white child-sized Bible with my name embossed in gold on the front, and I wasn't *saved*.

Every day the Christian school began and ended with the pledge of allegiance, the pledge to the Christian flag, and the first four verses of "Onward Christian Soldiers." Then Mrs. Green would become very quiet, turn toward the class, look into our little faces and call for any sinful child to come to the front, confess his transgressions before God and his classmates, and be saved.

All the other kids were professional Christians, having been previously saved at some earlier time in their five or six years on this earthly plane. Filled with the Holy Spirit, they turned and gazed in my direction. I sat sweating in my plaid jumper under a dark cloud of mortal sin.

I was a shy child by nature, and the thought of stepping forward during those grueling moments of silence seemed like an awful lot to ask. Plus, part of the deal was that in order to be saved the sinful child had to confess a list of hideous wrongdoings, and then drop to his or her knees, and pray for forgiveness. That done, the teacher would ask everyone to turn to a verse in their personalized Bibles, or in my case the loaner Bible for sinners which sat on Mrs. Green's desk, and we would read aloud a verse on redemption and pray together to get me a spot in the kingdom of heaven. I had a lot of work to do.

Weeks turned into months at the Christian school, and while other publicly educated first graders were struggling with the logic of phonics and the riddle of multiplication, planting sunflower seeds in cups and playing dodge ball at recess, my unfortunate classmates and I were busy recreating the terror of the fiery furnace with red and orange construction paper. We pieced together elaborate "sin collages" by carefully cutting out magazine pictures with our rounded safety scissors of people engaged in sinful acts—smoking, drinking, dancing, wearing pantyhose. We pasted the pictures onto poster board while reciting "the wages of sin is death."

I knew my parents were sinners. Sometimes on a weekend night my mother would smoke, drink, dance, *and* wear pantyhose all at the same time, but I felt rather lackluster in my sinfulness. I decided that if I was going to get up in front of the class and get myself saved, I needed to get some impressive stuff on my resume. I began to sin with a vengeance. I backtalked my parents, refused to eat vegetables, and spewed profanities at the drop of a hat. By Christmas, I was feeling mighty criminal and was ready, I believed, to be saved.

The last day before Christmas vacation was a short one, ending at noon. From my seat I could see the parents pulling into the circle drive at the front of the school, no doubt reaching for their own personalized Bibles to read from as they waited for their mini-Christians to be released into their care. I saw my mother's green Lincoln in the lineup, the window rolled down a crack to release a thin white plume of cigarette smoke. I snapped to attention as the class rose to its feet and began reciting its battery of pledges and hymns, and I prepared myself for redemption.

I stammered through the pledge of allegiance and the pledge to the Christian flag. By the time we were halfway through "Onward Christian Soldiers," I was a nervous wreck, and the room was beginning to spin. The prayer for sinners was a vibrating hum in my ears. I saw Mrs. Green motion to the sacred space between the flags and I knew my time of salvation was at hand.

I swallowed hard and ran full speed to the front of the classroom, grabbing the welfare Bible from the teacher's desk as I skidded past. I slid to my knees, nearly toppling Old Glory and the beloved Christian flag, squeezed my eyes shut, and let the sins fly.

"I pulled all the legs off a daddy longlegger; I said, 'God damn you, Grandma;' I spat green beans on the floor; and I poured cherry Kool-Aid all down the front of my sister's prom dress; I put my dad's shoes in the toilet and flushed it; and called my mom fat every day for two weeks." I opened my eyes slowly, hoping to see Mrs. Green and maybe even Jesus himself, with arms outstretched, ready to welcome me at last into the flock.

Mrs. Green clutched her own embossed Bible to her chest with one hand, her other hand covered her mouth. I imagined she was moved beyond words by my impassioned confession. She backed up a step, then put her hand on my arm and guided me away from the special place between the flags.

The rest of the class was excused for the day and Mrs. Green personally led me to my mother's car in the circle drive. I just knew that she was bursting with pride and couldn't wait to tell my mother the good news of my salvation. I was instructed to stand on the sidewalk and Mrs. Green stepped into my mother's car, waving at a cloud of cigarette smoke as she lowered herself into the passenger's seat.

I tried to look like I was examining my shoelace but I snuck peeks into the car and could see Mrs. Green wagging her Bible at my mother who flicked her cigarette out the window, then lit another one right away. Both of them took turns pointing at me and shaking their heads, and finally Mrs. Green burst out of the car and up the sidewalk without so much as a Merry Christmas and I scurried in to take her place in the long leather seat.

Mother threw the car into gear and we lurched away from the curb. She flicked her cigarette butt out the window again and I turned to see it glowing on the sidewalk where Mrs. Green and I had last stood.

"That Goddamned woman is as crazy as a loon!" Mother yelled. When she rounded the corner I had to hold onto the dash to keep myself upright. "Why didn't you tell me they were torturing you in there all this time?" She looked over at me and I could see there were tears in her eyes.

I stared out the window for a while—at the Atlas Grocery store and the post office whizzing past. We seemed to be going faster than usual, and Mother was talking a mile a minute. I didn't hear much of what she was saying, but I understood that I wouldn't be going back to the Christian school after Christmas break, or ever.

There was really only one thing on my mind. I waited for Mother to stop yelling long enough for me to ask the question that had been gnawing at me since I took the place in the sinner's circle between the flags. Scooting closer to Mother, now I was the one with tears in my eyes. I took a deep breath and managed to say in almost a whisper, "Did Mrs. Green tell you if I was *saved*?"

Mother slowed the car to a stop and looked down at my hands. I realized I was still clutching Mrs. Green's charity Bible and there were sweaty marks on its white leather surface. She pried the book from my fingers and set it behind me on the backseat as she pulled away from the curb. "Oh yes, Linda," she said as she checked the rearview mirror. "You are absolutely saved."

She Kept Fishes in an Old Iron Pan

Geraldo Valerio

MY UNCLE HAS A HUGE CAGE filled with all kinds of birds. It is as if he has all the birds of a forest inside this cage. They are many. There are little green birds called Grass Eaters. Grass Eaters do not eat grass but seeds of grass. There is also a tiny black bird that makes a short noise and then jumps in the air. He peeps and jumps. Peeps and jumps. There is another one that is blue. It is a dark blue bird. This bird is so dark blue that it is almost black. But when it comes close to you, you see its shadows and they are blue. There are also yellow canaries, white birds with rose beaks, and one that has black and white feathers on his body and whose head is completely red. There are yellow birds with blue and green feathers, brown birds with thick black beaks, birds with long legs, birds the size of chickens, and shy little doves.

But the bird that I like the most is a duck. It is a little duck with a little head and a short beak. For him, my uncle built a little pond inside the cage. The little duck spends most of his day swimming and this is what I enjoy the most about him. I never get tired of watching him swimming, paddling the water, diving his little head, and then shaking his wet feathers. I come to my uncle's house only to watch the little duck swim for me.

But I also like my uncle's house because he has a big yard full of fruit trees. A mango tree, a guava tree, and a peach tree.

My uncle Antonio is married to my mother's sister, Aunt Efigenia. Every time I come to their house, they buy me sweet bread. Sweet bread with coconut, sweet bread with cream, and sweet bread with sugar.

Before I leave for home, my aunt gives me coffee with sweet bread. She sets a table just for me. She serves me coffee in a large teacup and tells me I can put as much butter as I want on my bread. She also gives me a peach to take home with me. It is a pale green peach. Its skin is like velvet. My aunt tells me to peel it because the fur of its skin can hurt my mouth.

I say "ciao" and I leave with my peach. I stop at the bird's cage once more and watch the duck swimming.

I feel uneasy after watching so many birds. I want to have all of them, but Dad says it isn't a good idea to have so many birds at home, because they will bring bugs with them.

Coming home, I am still thinking about the birds. I walk around the yard trying to imagine where I can build my big cage with a little pond inside. But then I remember that birds have bugs.

I leave the house and wander around until I come to the river. There are many bushes of tall grass along the river. There I see a group of Grass Eaters. They fly fast and they stay close together all the time. When they fly around the bushes, they look like a green moving cloud.

They fly along the river and stop at the bushes to feed on the seeds. They peep loud. They eat and peep and when I come close to them they fly away to the other side of the river like a flying peeping cloud.

There at the riverbed I meet my friend Regina. She is catching little fishes. My friend catches many of them and she keeps them in an old iron pan.

My friend lives in a house with a huge backyard, filled with all kinds of trees. Mangoes, guavas, bananas, and some others trees that I don't know the names of. That yard is so big, that at the end, when you think it is the end, there is still a vast area. This place is completely different from the rest of the yard.

This place is a big pigpen. There, there is a house for an immense female pig that always has lots of little pigs sucking her teats. She is a beautiful pig. She looks like a mountain of soft flesh with many noisy and hungry little pigs around her. She is fat because when she is not sleeping, she is eating. She has a strong smell, like only pigs have. Little pigs walk on their tiptoes and swing their tails all the time.

In the middle of the pigpen, there is a mulberry tree. Mulberries are purple, sweet, and juicy. The mulberry tree has long branches that bend to the floor. Sometimes, the mulberries are so ripe and soft that they cannot be touched without making our fingers purple. Ripe mulberries make your tongue and gums purple. Ripe mulberries are sweet. Grandma said they are food for birds.

My friend doesn't like to share her mulberries with me. She is the kind of friend who, even though she has many fruit trees in her yard, will never give you anything, and if she does, she will chose the one that is half eaten by the birds or flies. She says: *There is nothing wrong with this guava. You only have to take out the bad part and eat the good.*

The mango trees at her house are high and climbing high trees can be really hard. If you climb them, it doesn't mean you will be able to climb down. Climbing down is the hardest part. Climbing down and falling down can easily be the same. Sometimes in a tree you find yourself not knowing \ what to do or how to do it.

My friend knows how to climb her trees. She walks up the tree, finds its fruit and eats some, throws down the seed and peels. Because I never can go as high as she can, I never find mangoes and I never eat them, and she never brings one for me. She says: *If you cannot find them yourself, I won't do it for you.*

She climbs down the tree with her mouth yellow and her teeth filled with yellow strings. For a few minutes she stops to clean her teeth with her black dirt nails and says: *That was good.*

I remember that Mom told me we should not clean our teeth in front of other people. I think it is time to go back home. I wonder if I should ever come back here.

But my friend has a big iron pan filled with fishes. I am trying to get her to give me some and she never decides what to do. She says: *I will think about it.*

Then she says she has a great idea. I love great ideas and I follow her. She says she wants to play with fire and I also like playing with fire.

We make a little fire and she puts some stones around it and says: *Now I am going to boil the water and see how the fish swim in hot water.*

The fishes, they don't swim. They die as soon as the water gets hot. The water is already boiling when I think it would have been better to go back home.

At home I find my green peach.

Mom peels it for me. She says we should peel the fruit with care, taking thin strips and saving as much flesh as we can. She quietly peels the peach. She says that if we had enough peaches, she would make a jelly. She tells me you only need sugar, water, some cloves, cinnamon, and peaches. You make syrup with water, sugar, and spices, and you let the fruit cook for some time over a low fire. She says it tastes really good. She tells me that she is going to make some for me some day. I wonder if we should save the peach in order to make a jelly. She says it would be a better idea to eat it.

The peeled peach is pale green. Now I can see also some different colors. It is a pale green with shades of yellow and orange.

Mom slices the peach and we both eat it. It is bitter, a little bit sour and hard. It feels good.

Normal People With Belly Buttons

Ariel Gore

THE PRIEST WAS SUPPOSED TO BE A SECRET.

The front door opened and the floorboards creaked after Leslie and I had gone to bed. If he was still there in the morning, asleep on the black and white checkered pullout couch-bed, we couldn't tell anyone.

The priest looked ancient to me, gray hair thinning behind his ears, deep laugh lines around his eyes. He was bald on top except for a wispy tuft of hair that stuck straight up in the middle. In my illustrations of *The Last Supper*, Jesus became the priest and he was a smiling pumpkin head. That wispy tuft of hair became a green-brown vine.

We'd never been Catholics before, but now we went to morning Mass and afternoon Mass and we washed our sins away in the silver bowl of water at the entrance to St. Anne's Chapel. Now we took and ate, this was the body of Christ. Now we took and drank, this was the bittersweet blood of Our Savior.

The priest wore a long white robe and a red and orange Guatemalan stole. When everyone stood to recite the Lord's Prayer, I stared up at the stained glass crucifixion scene. All the people in the congregation whispered the strange mantra, riding their f's and their s's, and the whole prayer ran together like a single word: *Ourffffatherwhoartinheaven…* I moved my lips to remember the sounds, but I was silent. Then we all traced triangles from our foreheads to our shoulder to our other shoulder: *Inthenameofffftheffffatherthessssonandtheholyssssspirit.*

"WHERE DOES GOD LIVE?" I asked the Priest. I was perched at the foot of the black and white checked pullout couch-bed in the living room, holding my little blue tambourine at my side.

"Oh—," the priest sat up, surprised to see me there. "God lives everywhere," he said.

I could hear the shower running in the bathroom. "Does he live in this house?"

"Yes, of course," the priest assured me.

"Does he live in that tree?" I pointed out the window to the old oak that had my swing hanging from it.

The priest twisted his body around to look. "Yes, certainly. God lives in that tree."

"Does he live in this tambourine?" I gave the thing a shake so it jingled.

"Yes. God lives everywhere," the priest said.

"What shape is God?"

"God is no shape," The priest pushed his blanket aside and swung his long legs over the edge of the bed. He was wearing red long-johns.

"God has to be some shape. Square, circle?"

"God isn't one particular shape," the priest told me. "God is all around us. Everywhere, in everything."

"I'll bet he's a triangle," I said. I was thinking of the father, the son, and the Holy Spirit. Or maybe I was thinking of my mother, my father, and the priest. I set my tambourine down on the floor and tip-toed back into the bedroom. I fished around in my big wicker toy chest for my steel triangle and the metal stick that went with it.

Leslie peered over the edge of her top bunk. "Whatcha looking for?"

"My triangle." I found it under a neglected handmade China doll and brought it out to the living room to show the priest.

He was dressed now and replacing the cushions on the checkered couch.

"Here." I held the triangle up by its cord and hit a high note that lingered in the air. "Is that God?"

"Yes," he said as he sat down on the couch and folded his hands in his lap.

I thought maybe the priest had a bright flame hidden behind his eyes because his whole face glowed when he smiled. So I had it. God was a triangle. "Why don't you wear a black priest suit?"

He wore a cardigan sweater, like Mr. Rogers. "I was never terribly comfortable in my cassock," he said. "Haven't worn it for years."

"But you're supposed to wear it, aren't you?"

"Phooey on 'supposed to,'" the priest said.

"Phooey on poohy," I said, giving the triangle a good whack. "Phooey on poohy!"

The priest cleared his throat. "You don't say."

"Did Adam and Eve have bellybuttons?" I lifted up my shirt to show the priest mine.

The priest clucked his tongue as he pulled on his socks. "Well now, *ha*, obviously they wouldn't need them, would they? The Bible doesn't say, but most of the art shows them looking like normal people."

"Normal people with bellybuttons?"

"Well, you see, Adam and Eve are mythological creatures, so you can picture them any way you like. Before people knew about biology, they had to make up stories to explain things to themselves."

"If they had bellybuttons, do you think they were in-ies or out-ies?"

But before the priest could answer me, the doorbell rang and my mother came rushing out of the bathroom, pulling on the flowered dress that made all the kids on the block call us Gypsies. "Shit," my mother muttered.

The priest stood up, confused and panicked, held his large hands up in the air.

I pushed him into the living room closet.

My mother nudged the door open just a crack to see who was there.

Leslie shuffled in from our bedroom, rubbing her eyes. She climbed onto the couch, looked out the window to see who it was. She shook her head, glanced around the room. She grabbed the priest's glasses from the table next to the couch, slipped them into the pocket of her gold Chinese robe, then pointed at the giant slippers in the corner of the room and I kicked them under the couch. "Don't say anything stupid," Leslie warned me.

"We're doing wonderfully," my mother was telling the person at the door. "Thanks so much for stopping by. We should get together for lunch sometime soon—"

I could tell that my mother was trying to wrap up the conversation, but the caller was persistent.

"Oh, yes," my mother said. "The girls are still in their pajamas, but do come in—"

The blue-haired lady from church followed my mother inside and wrinkled her nose at me when I hit my triangle. She had a big black purse she held tight at her side.

My mother gestured towards our bedroom, "The girls sleep in there—" then led our inquisitive guest into the kitchen.

The blue-haired lady didn't say much, just sniffed around the corners of our house. My mother had told me about the witch who tattled on the priest's brother when he was a priest, too. Witches came snooping after rumors and tattled on the priests when they snuck out at night to see *Harold and Maude* and didn't come back to their rooms until morning. I was sure the blue-haired lady was a witch, with her big black purse and her pointy nose.

"It really was so sweet of you to stop by," my mother said, smiling too wide. "So sweet, really." Her voice seemed to be getting higher and higher.

I thought I heard the priest cough in the closet, so I gave my triangle a hard whack. I felt sorry for him, crouched there in the dark with our winter coats.

The blue-haired lady wrinkled her nose at me again. "Good day, then," she said as she left.

We watched from the window as she drifted down the walkway clutching her big purse, glanced back, and then disappeared.

My mother was laughing when she opened the closet door, but the priest looked rattled, his little tuft of hair slightly askew.

Leslie handed him his glasses.

He nodded, smiled his jack-o-lantern smile, and slipped out the back.

SUNDAY MORNING WE WASHED away our sins in the silver bowl of water at the entrance to the chapel. We'd never been baptized, but the priest had told us himself that it didn't matter. We were born pure and were pure still, our bodies temples of the Holy Spirit. The priest stood by the door in his long white robe. "Good morning, Father," the parishioners all said as they filed past. The priest smiled at my mother. She was wearing her Sunday red bandana and big gold-hoop earrings.

"Good morning, Father," I cooed up at the priest. I wore the blue cotton dress my Grandma gave me. It had ruffles at the collar and matching blue bloomers I wore underneath.

"Good morning, Chickadee," he whispered.

I sat in the pew at the back of the church between Leslie and my mother while a woman up near the altar strummed her acoustic guitar, singing *Moonshadow*. Jesus hung on his cross in the stained-glass window, two women crying at his feet. His blood dripped down from his palms like a warning. *Here's what can happen.*

"Let us pray," the priest began from the pulpit.

And I prayed to my triangular god that soon the priest would be my father for real.

The Little Delicate One

Helena Carlson

I WAS ASTONISHED and delighted when my tall grown up handsome cousin Jack O'Reilly suddenly appeared by my hospital bed, scooped me up in his arms, and dashed down a long wide flight of marble stairs out into the freedom of the Dublin streets. "I'm here to rescue you, kiddo. My car is outside and we'll be home safe in no time," he said.

I had given up hope of ever escaping from my long and painful stay in the Adelaide Hospital. He put me gently into the front seat of his car and drove recklessly all the way home. I was thrilled to the core.

Three months earlier, shortly after my eighth birthday, in a freak accident in our new home, I'd been badly burned. Our house was so new that the gas and electricity had not yet been turned on and my mother had to make do with heating water and cooking over the fireplace. I was sitting on the floor in front of the fire, happily trying on a new pair of shoes, when the pot of boiling water fell from the hob. The sooty bottom of the pot hit my foot and scalding water poured out over the floor. The pain was excruciating and I screamed and ran wildly from room to room, trying to escape the blistering pain. I ran so fast that my mother had difficulty catching me.

When frightened, my mother felt helpless. She wasn't a fighter and had learned to be the peacemaker in the family—especially when dealing with my volatile father. She picked me up and ran next door to our new neighbor for help. My mother thought the neighbor was a nurse, but she was instead a dimwitted countrywoman who in her ignorance poured linseed oil over my foot in an attempt to ease the frightful pain and heal the wound. Of course, my mother knew no better, but we always blamed the woman next door for the ensuing damage. The linseed oil treatment caused a serious infection and worsened my injury.

My father rushed home and immediately took charge. He shouted, "She needs to see a doctor at once!"

We didn't have a car, so father sat me on the cross bar of his bicycle and peddled furiously several miles to the doctor's house.

When the doctor examined my foot, he exclaimed, "My God, man, what have you put on her foot?"

"Our neighbor said linseed oil was a good country treatment for burns so she poured some on Helena's foot," father replied nervously.

The doctor looked horrified. "That is the worst thing you can do to an injury like this."

He put on some kind of soothing jelly and gingerly wrapped my foot in gauze. He gave my father some medicine to take home and said, "The visiting nurse will come daily to change the dressings." He left his surgery still grumbling about the stupidity of some people.

At home I was in great pain as I lay in bed. They put a big wire cage over my foot and leg to avoid the bedclothes touching my foot. I fell asleep but would wake up if I moved. My buttocks were also painfully scalded, but fortunately had not received the linseed oil treatment because I was too shy to mention my sore bottom.

I was always terrified of going to any hospital, but I was told that I would have to go there since my foot was not getting any better. I screamed that I would not go. My mother held me close and tried to reassure me about this special hospital. She sought to calm me by describing a paradise for children in this wonderful hospital.

"They will let you listen to *The Children's Hour* all day. You know you love that radio program and the wonderful stories they tell. In this hospital all the children get to eat Fuller's chocolate cake for every meal. Your daddy and I will visit you every day."

So the ambulance took me away.

I was put in an isolation room as soon as I got there because of the fear of infection from such burns. I do not remember being admitted and must have fallen asleep, which I was doing more often. Later, I found out that the doctor told my mother that the wound was very bad and hinted that amputation might be a possibility. My mother was horrified. My parents were allowed to come to a small window in the isolation room and look in at me but could not come to my bedside.

The treatment for burns and scalds was primitive in those days, before antibiotics became freely available. The basic treatment was debraiding, which involved the cutting away of infected tissue to prevent the spread of infection in the wound. I did not understand anything except that the doctor and nurse every day would torture me for no reason. I hated them. Every day a nurse would appear pulling a trolley with all kinds of instruments of torture. I screamed with fear and fought as hard as I could to prevent them from touching me. "Stop your crying now," she'd say sharply. "We have to do this to get you better. Here, hold these bandages for me. You can roll them up."

She was trying to distract me from what was coming. I would start rolling bandages, but at the first pain I'd throw them at the nurse. Finally, when I still struggled, she lay over my body to restrain me while the doctor removed my gauze bandages and started cutting away the dead tissue from my foot. The pain was savage when they cut live tissue as they tried to remove damaged burned skin. I do not remember receiving any anesthetic.

I was eventually released from isolation and put into the children's ward. Time crawled slowly by and still my parents never visited me. No one visited me. I could see the other mothers and fathers visiting and bringing presents for their children. I felt totally abandoned and very lonely. I missed my family terribly. It was weeks before I managed to climb down from my bed and gingerly lower myself to the floor. The floor was highly polished and the ambulatory kids loved to slide and sort of skate up and down the center aisle. It was a very big room and they had great fun skittering across the slick floors. When nurses came back into the children's' ward, they all scampered back into their beds again, but they were never punished for playing. I had a heavily bandaged foot and could not stand up. But I could lie on my back on the floor and the other kids would grab me by my nightgown and pull me ever faster across the floor. I loved that sense of motion. They raced wildly up and down, laughing their heads off at the funny little girl they were pulling. I spread my arms wide and felt like I was flying through the air. When they let go, I slid under a bed. I was enormously pleased that the kids would play with me. It was all very exciting.

When Christmas came, the nurses, in a spirit of fairness, took all the presents brought in for children and then portioned them out so that every child got at least one present. This was an Irish kind of communism. I do not remember what I received but I do remember that I thought it was a poor excuse for a Christmas present. However, the girl in the next bed received a big paper-maché Donald Duck full of sweets. I knew it was expensive and I watched her enviously.

"Mary, could I just play a little bit with Donald? I will be very careful with him," I said.

All the sweets had been devoured by then and she had generously given me some of the toffees. But I wanted to hold the toy just for a while. She passed it over to me. I cuddled it and explored it carefully. Then I noticed writing on the bottom of the duck and read the words with shock. It said: "To Helena, Merry Christmas, Love from Mammy and Daddy."

It really was *my* toy. My parents had not abandoned me after all. They had sent in a lovely Christmas present for me. My joy was soon followed by a sense of raging injustice that my toy had been given to another kid. There was no use howling about it. The nurses would stand for no nonsense from any of us, so I quietly fumed and harbored resentment toward generous Mary.

JACK'S SUDDEN ARRIVAL was like an archangel descending from heaven to release me. When I got home my mother and father showered me with love. I enjoyed being coddled in the big armchair next to the warm fire. My mother cried when she saw my badly scarred foot but my pragmatic father said, "Well, it's better than a wooden foot. She'll get better in time. She'll soon be running around with the other kids. Then we can start worrying again."

Much later I found the courage to ask my mother why they never visited me in hospital. I thought that I had been too bold a girl to deserve any visits. "Mammy, why didn't you and Daddy come to see me in the hospital? All the other kids had visitors."

"We did come to see you as soon as you were admitted," she said. "But you started screaming and crying and begging to be taken home. The doctor told us that it would be better if we didn't visit you because it upset you too much. He did let us look at your through a window in the isolation room, but that was all."

"But Mammy, I missed you and I was so lonely. If I could have seen you I wouldn't have cried so much." I felt relieved to find out that they actually had come, and I blamed those dreadful torturers in the hospital for my loneliness.

Because of my three-month hospital stay, I had become extremely thin and frail. My grandmother used to put an Irish penny across my wrist to dramatically show the neighbors how thin I was. The penny was wider than my wrist. My twin was rosy cheeked and healthy. That was when neighbors started referring to me as *"the little delicate one."*

I actually gloried in the attention and soon found out in school that being *"the little delicate one"* had advantages. One day when I behaved boldly, I was dragged out to see the Mother Superior for a caning. The nun looked at me and said, "I can't hit that little delicate one. I will give her twin four slaps of the cane and that will frighten this one enough to make her behave." My poor twin never forgave me for that.

The family went on a mission to feed me up into health and also protect me from the harsh Irish winter. The doctor told my mother to buy me shoes of the softest leather to protect the thin skin on my injured foot. She haunted Dublin shoe stores and finally found a pair as soft as glove leather. Unfortunately, they were also pointy toed and a bright yellow color. I hated them on sight and swore I would never wear them. I was now nine years old and feared the ridicule and cruelty of children towards any odd looking child. I screamed at my mother: "Those are women's shoes. All the kids will laugh at me. I will never wear them. I won't go out in them."

I cried to no avail and I had to put on the hated shoes. Then my beautiful mother decided that I had to be kept warm, so she sacrificed her favorite possession from America. She cut down her gorgeous sleek sealskin coat into a smaller coat for me. She was not a good seamstress, and the coat was odd looking and ill-fitting. She sewed new red buttons down the front of the cut-down coat and the coat became a sort of clown outfit. I cried harder. "I hate women's clothes. I hate women's shoes. All the kids will laugh at me. I will never go outside dressed like that."

Matters were worsened because I was such a small, pale, skinny kid. I must have looked like a nervous mouse peering out from my stiff shiny black sealskin coat with the red buttons and wearing pointy toed yellow women's shoes. I was an instant hit with all the kids who hooted and laughed and pointed at me. No other kid in all Dublin was ever sent out to play dressed so extraordinarily. I skulked around, hiding behind anything I could. I couldn't run fast yet, so I was frequently trapped by a bunch of jeering kids.

It seemed ages before I could dress in ordinary clothes and shoes again and join the kids in jeering some other poor unfortunate child.

A Family History

Adrian Shirk

IN 1976, A TWENTY-YEAR-OLD woman and her boyfriend were going
to school right outside Portland, Oregon. They both studied music. One
weekend they drove three hours to Seattle so she could introduce him to
her parents. I imagine her mother waited on the smooth, cement front
porch with a gin and tonic for everyone. It was an off-white bungalow with
piles of nameless junk beginning to steadily fill in the front drive. There
were apple trees and lots of flowers and pots of Aloe Vera spiraling off the
steps. They all sipped their drinks at the kitchen table. The sun showed
through the various colored vases on the window sill, including the royal
blue one in the shape of The Virgin. The boyfriend had noticed a stack of
new roof shingles on the front porch when they first arrived. At some
point he inquired about it to his girlfriend's father. The father probably
grumbled about the inconvenience of the rain and how he was going to get
around to it. The boyfriend remembered seeing an industrial tarp draped
across a section of the house top. The father crossed his arms, sliding his

bottom lip out in quick spasms, adjusting his hip. The mother made another drink, chuckling and twisting her long, graying hair into something more manageable.

Two years later, the twenty-year-old woman and her boyfriend were married.

First they had my brother. They lived in a house across the street from my grandparents in Seattle. My mom taught music therapy and played the flute. My dad drove a bus and played the trombone. Maybe they were happy. If they weren't, I don't know why they had another one. Because then they moved to Brooklyn, New York and had me. Musician Union strikes and co-op daycares and a small house by Lake Washington that could have changed the course of our lives if we had chosen to stay. In 1992, when I was four years old, they got divorced. Within six years they'd both re-married and started new families. My mother and father were together for fourteen years and they almost never talked again.

The stack of roof shingles sat on my grandparents' front porch for twenty-six years. My grandpa fashioned more and more tarps as time went on to keep the Northwest weather out. The steadily building piles of junk built their way around the house. My grandma moved out without a word. Her hair turned bright silver. We visited my grandpa while he was living alone. He spent most of his time in a tower at the top of the house, following the stock market. The junk was at an all-time high and there were fruit flies everywhere.

My grandma lived wordlessly away for three years. In 2002, my grandpa paid someone to fix the roof and a few other things. She moved wordlessly back in. They painted their house orange and green. Now they make gin and tonics everyday, sipping them at their kitchen table with all the same vases casting all the same light.

Rocky Horror Virgins

Rachael Duke

IT'S 11:00 P.M. ON A WARM SPRING SATURDAY when Anne Foster and I sneak out of her house to see the *Rocky Horror Picture Show* at the Graceland Shopping Center. We quietly put on our shoes, grab our school *wildcat* jackets we brought upstairs earlier, and slip through the kitchen door. The dinner dishes, washed and dried by Anne's mother, are still stacked on the kitchen counter. They glisten in the moonlight like large pastel candies.

The night is perfect—slightly cool and sweet smelling, the big trees in Anne's neighborhood stretch their branches up to a cloudless sky with blinking stars and half a moon, and we can hear the sound of our shoes as we walk along the sidewalk. Unlike my neighborhood, the houses here don't all look exactly the same.

"We have to be at Jennifer's in ten minutes," Anne says. "You should see the car her mom got her. It has this really great sound system."

When we get there, Jennifer is waiting outside on her front porch.

She's dressed up like a bloodthirsty French maid, with her hair teased into a frizzy black cloud, a tiny white lacy hat, and an apron over a little black dress. Her face is painted white and her lips are exceptionally red. "I am so psyched you guys, let's go," she whispers loudly, looking up once at the big window over the driveway. "The guys are already in the car."

I look in the back seat and see Jeff Kayate, Dave Tyus, and Todd Alexander. They take up the entire back seat, so Anne and I open the door and get in the front.

"You guys are late," Kayate says.

"No we're not," I answer.

"Shut up," says Jennifer. "Let's get out of here before my parents wake up." And she puts the car in neutral and backs out of the driveway without even turning on the engine.

"You guys have to push," she says to the back seat.

"Come on, woman's lib, why don't you get Anne and Rachael to push?" Kayate answers. Dave and Todd both crack up at this. Anne and I look at each other. We are both thinking what idiots these guys are.

"Fine," Anne says, and I open the door.

"One, two, three," I whisper and we both push as hard as we can. Jennifer is at the front pushing, with her door open. The guys are in the back practically doubled over with laughter. I'm surprised when the car actually moves. We push it for a whole block before Jennifer leaps back in the car and starts the engine. Then we climb back in the front seat.

Todd starts singing between giggles, "I am woman, hear me roar!" He wears big metal glasses and is the only black kid in Anne's neighborhood. Everyone in the car lives in this neighborhood but me.

The place we usually hang is Jeff's house, and Todd lives right next door. Todd is a year younger than us, but he's funny and smart when he isn't acting like a jerk. His older sister used to baby-sit Anne, and Anne's mom still has this picture of Anne and Todd from when they were six and playing in one of those little plastic pools at Todd's house. Anne says it's completely embarrassing, but her mom refuses to take it down.

Jeff Kayate is the only guy I know who has his own place. It's right behind his family's house, a white farm house still left standing in an otherwise normal neighborhood. His apartment is one big room on top of another room that we call The Shed. To get to Kayate's you have to climb up a lot of wooden stairs that are outside the building and a little slippery in the rain. Inside is a television, a couch, a water bed, a stereo that plays a whole lot of Billy Joel, and a kitchen that no one ever uses, except to store *Rolling Rock* and *Genesee Cream Ale*. Kayate still eats inside with his family since he's only fifteen, like me.

We spend a lot of time in The Shed. The Shed is filled with overstuffed furniture and another sound system. Kayate and Todd make a lot of jokes about bringing girls there. When Anne and I are there we just drink beer and hang around.

Anne lives on the next block. Her dad is a Methodist minister and her mom puts wheat germ in everything she makes, including cookies. Her family holds hands and sings before dinner and they eat slowly and talk without fighting.

Anne nudges me in the car. "Look at this." She pulls down the neckline of her shirt and I can see the shadow of a bright red hickey. The boys are too busy making themselves laugh to notice.

"Where'd you get it?"

"Orchestra workshop Wednesday night." Anne plays cello and this exposes her to a lot more than classical music. I wonder how she has time to play music at all. I have never had a hickey. I haven't really had a real boyfriend yet either. I'm not sure which comes first.

"Who's been here before?" Jennifer yells.

"I have," Dave says.

Anne and I exchange surprised looks. "Really?"

"Yeah, my dad's wife took me like six months ago or something. It's all right."

Dave is the quietest and shyest of any of us, and he's recently become a born-again, so he doesn't spend a lot of time hanging out with us anymore. He has all these meetings and social events. This is something we don't talk about too much with him. Only once so far has he tried to convert me: "Come on Rachael," he said to me once over the phone. "I don't want you to burn in hell. I'm worried about you." In the background I could hear his dad, a famous local jazz musician, practicing drums.

"Just *all right?*" Jennifer shrieks. "Come on—it's great."

"Yeah," Dave says. "I probably shouldn't of come."

"Oh, come on man." Kayate hits him lightly on the leg. "It's cool. It's not like we're going to do anything but watch the movie. Jennifer's not going to molest you or anything. We'll protect your virtue."

"Shut up asshole," Jennifer says.

We drive with our windows down. Rush plays loud on the stereo, each guy in the back scrapping for enough space to play a large air guitar. I've never been out with my friends this late before without a parent. I feel happy all the way to my fingernails.

The Graceland Shopping Center is an extremely big parking lot surrounded by a lot of stores, a movie theater, and a Farrell's ice cream parlor. Sometimes my mom will drive me and Anne here and we'll see a movie and get ice cream. But tonight, when we get there, Farrell's is already closed and there's a line outside the movie theater. Half the people waiting are dressed up in crazy outfits like Jennifer. Someone is selling small plastic bags of rice. It's like a Halloween party in May.

"I think some of these people come every week," Jennifer says as we get in line. She's looking around and smoothing her skirt down so that it covers as much of her as possible, which isn't a lot.

Eventually a guy dressed up in black tights, a sequin shirt open to his belly button, a fake afro, and lots of makeup comes over to Jennifer. "These your friends?"

"Yeah. Hey you guys, this is Luke. He goes to Central."

"Hey man," Kayate says. Todd and Dave just nod. They're trying to figure this guy out. They would never dress up like that.

"Hey," I say.

He puts his arm around Jennifer for a moment, then runs off. "I'll see you later. Have fun you Rocky Horror Virgins," he calls to us.

Kayate holds up his hand without saying anything. Todd snickers. Dave shakes his head.

Todd looks at us and says, "Well, you virgins, can anyone loan me five bucks? I left my money at home."

Kayate rolls his eyes and hands him some money as the line starts moving.

The movie is pretty bizarre—a straight couple meets up with these people who seem to have a lot of sex and one is a little like a really buff Frankenstein. Plus there is a lot of music and everyone in the audience kind of acts out certain parts of the story and does some dancing. I sit between Anne and Dave. Anne and I are laughing about a lot of it, and it's wild to watch everyone there.

After the movie the lights come on I can see that the theater is completely trashed. Not just food containers everywhere, but beer bottles and rice from the wedding scene. When we get outside Jennifer is craning her neck around, probably looking for Luke, who doesn't materialize.

"That was cool," Anne says. "I loved the part where the guys says, *Come in, it's raining.*"

"I thought it was weird," Kayate grins. "But I liked the part where that girl was singing, *Touch me, creature of the night.*"

Todd laughs and Dave is quiet. Then Dave visibly takes a big breath and says, "I just don't think it was right."

"What?" Anne says.

"All that sex stuff, plus that guy was you know, *gay* or something."

"Whatever. He wasn't gay, he was a *transvestite.* You know, a guy who dresses up like a girl," says Jennifer.

"Well, that's fucked up," Todd says.

"You guys are so stupid," I say. "You missed the point of the whole movie. It's supposed to be fun."

"Yeah," says Jennifer, looking at the guys. "Were you offended by the outer space part too?"

"That was just weird," Kayate says.

We stop at Jennifer's car and no one says anything. We can hear people talking and laughing in the parking lot as they get in their cars and take off. Mostly they're older than us. We stand there, all six of us, just kind of staring at each other and not sure what to say.

"Are you sure this is your car?" I ask. I look at the bumper that I'd pushed silently down the street a couple of hours earlier and it looks different. I put my hand on the cool metal. Usually someone would've made fun of me for asking such a stupid question. But we're all dazed.

"Yeah, and we gotta go," Jennifer says. "The cops come by to make sure people aren't partying in the parking lot when the movie gets out."

Jennifer unlocks the driver's side, gets in, and then unlocks all the other doors. We sit in the same seats as before and Anne turns on the radio as Jennifer pulls out of the parking lot. We sing along at the top of our lungs with the windows down, the dark spring night surrounding us, the passing lights of cars illuminating parts of our faces. I almost feel like we're still in the movie, getting ready to go to outer space.

When we get back to Jennifer's house, she cuts the engine before pulling into the driveway, and this time the guys make a big deal of getting out of the car and pushing. Then we walk back, past Anne's house to The Shed. It's pitch black outside until Kayate turns on the light outside the shed. While we sit on the grass outside, Kayate goes in and turns on the music, not too loud since it is 2:00 A.M. We dance on the grass. First it's a slow song, and Todd grabs my waist, not too smooth or graceful, and we dance. He feels sweaty but I put my arms around his neck and dance with him anyway.

After a few minutes the song is over and the next song is heavy metal *Highway to Hell*. Kayate pushes it up a little louder, and there we are, dancing like individual whirlwinds on his lawn, under the night sky, each of us our own little planet in a giant galaxy. Jennifer's hat has fallen off, and Anne stomps her feet. All three guys play air guitar, their heads thrown back and their arms slightly elevated like they have some kind of offering.

This is my tribe, I think, my heart beating with the music, the sky spinning above me. Each of us is alone, but we're all together, and I know it won't get much better than this.

Mistake

Amanda Risser

I PICK UP a chart and read the information that the paramedics gathered about this patient when they picked him up at his apartment downtown: *laceration, left forearm.* I'm relieved. Maybe the guy just needs stitches. That would be straightforward, satisfying. A discrete endpoint. A job well done. I have been sewing and knitting ever since I can remember and stitching together edges of flesh is familiar and soothing. I read on: *20-year-old male. Had argument with girlfriend earlier this evening, went into other room and cut his arm with kitchen knife. Girlfriend called 911, she says he jumped off a Bridge in July.*

"Shit!" I say aloud to the clipboard. The ward clerk laughs at me from behind her desk as she dispatches a canister of blood to the lab through the pneumatic tube—*kathunk, swoosh.*

"Rough night?"

"Rough fifteen months." That's exactly how long my residency has been so far. I've been working eighty- to 110-hour weeks for the past seven months with overnight call twice a week. I'm in the middle of my month of ER night shift, twelve- to fourteen-hour nights starting at 8:00 P.M. I come home every morning, crawl into bed, pull the curtains, sleep all day in the summer heat, wake up, go to work, do it all over again.

I have some time to see someone new so I head in to see this laceration guy before rounding on my other patients. I get caught up in the privacy drape hanging behind the sliding glass door to his room. I feel— for the hundredth time since I started working here—like a third grader in a school play getting all tangled up in the theater curtains only to stumble on stage to the laughter of an audience of parents. I feel like my costume hat is all crooked and I can't remember my lines. "Hi. I'm Dr. Risser, one of the docs working in the ER tonight. I understand you cut yourself, is that right?"

"Yes ma'am."

I have to lean forward to hear him. His voice is quiet and flat and the "ma'am" feels wrong for the situation. He looks like a normal college student—intentionally scruffy beard, dark, hip, second-hand clothing. He looks at me with extremely pale blue eyes and now he's leaning slightly forward.

All of a sudden I want to get out of here, away from him. I'm thinking about how in some cultures, and with dogs, direct eye contact is threatening. I stare back at him to try and establish some authority, but I can't. I finally look down, trying to pass it off like its time to check out his wound. "Well, let's take a look."

"Yes, ma'am."

I remove the gauze and see a gaping wound four inches long, fat visible at the base. Not bleeding too much, straight edge. Should be easy to sew up. "So what happened when you did this to yourself? Did you want to hurt yourself or kill yourself?"

"I'm not sure, ma'am. I didn't mean to hurt myself, ma'am." His voice continues to be quiet, hard to hear above the nurses laughing outside the room, the drunk guy moaning next door in between retches.

"What was going on in your head when this happened?"

"Not much of anything, ma'am."

"Were you angry? Were you sad? What kinds of feelings went along with this?"

"I'm not sure, ma'am."

His answers are slow, each one punctuated by "ma'am" like I'm a drill sergeant in the suicidal army. His face is still—no emotion. He keeps looking at me just a little too hard with those creepy pale eyes.

"Are you depressed?" I try.

"No, ma'am."

"Did you get in a fight with your girlfriend?"

"No, ma'am. I'm just anxious about school starting tomorrow, that's all. I need to get enough sleep tonight before classes start." He smiles and makes a small movement with his uncut hand, gesturing to the room around him. "This doesn't help much, being here."

A weird variation on the common ER theme of *can you speed things up, doc? I've been here five hours already and I'll miss work tomorrow.* The guy slashes himself and now wants speedy service so that he can get out of here. I feel myself becoming rigid, my voice hardening. "Well, yeah, but you know this is kind of a big deal and we've got some things to sort out here. This isn't the first time you've done something like this, right? What about this summer on the bridge?"

His eyes widen a little in surprise. Maybe he didn't know his girlfriend shared this information with the paramedics. "I *swear* I didn't want to hurt myself, ma'am."

I'm starting to lose patience as I think about the other folks I'm tending to out there. "I think most people would agree that jumping off a bridge is expressing a pretty clear intention to harm yourself. So is cutting your arm deep enough so that I can see the fat there." I point out his fat to him with my purple-gloved finger for emphasis. "So what's going on, are you hearing voices or something?" I think back to when I was a medical student and when I was learning about how to talk to people about their issues respectfully, calmly, empathetically. I'm pretty sure what I just said would be a great example of "The Wrong Way." Well, fuck it.

"No, ma'am." He replies.

"OK, well, I'm gonna go get some supplies ready and you need to be on a psychiatric hold since we consider you to be a harm to yourself right now, OK?" I sigh and get all the paperwork together, ask the clerk to set him up with a someone to sit in the room to watch him, and read him the legal statement on the hold papers and get him to sign.

He asks to make a call. His 'sitter' goes with him and he stands at the payphone by the nurses' station whispering into the mouthpiece. I notice that his feet are bare and spattered with dried blood.

I go see my other patients. I peek in on Mrs. Smith. She is slumped over in her bed, her leg hanging over the side. She had a stroke two weeks ago and can't speak. Tonight she started throwing up blood at her new nursing home. She's got dried blood on her mouth, nose, and teeth. We're sending her to the intensive care unit and we're just watching her until they come fetch her. The notes from her recent admission say that she'd been an active and independent older lady prior to her stroke, and that was just two weeks ago. I lean down and push the hair out of her eyes, squeeze her hand. I think of how things can change so fast and wonder what she was like before the stroke. "You're going to the ICU, OK? They'll take really good care of you there and hopefully you'll be out soon."

She nods and I move on to the next room.

Next door is the Spanish-speaking family, parents to a two-month-old with a fever. Luckily, I speak Spanish pretty well so I tell them that the chest X-ray, urinalysis, and blood tests don't show anything.

They look relieved. "So it's nothing, then?"

I explain that, in this case, finding nothing is actually a problem. That tiny babies' immune systems can't contain infections like in older people, that bacteria could be hiding in his blood or even the fluid that surrounds his brain and spinal cord. I've already explained and negotiated blood tests, a chest X-ray and a catheter sample of his urine and now have to explain that the next step is to take fluid from his back and test it.

I look down at the baby; he has an impressive head of shiny black hair and a cowlick that makes it stick straight up in front. He's wrapped in a fuzzy pink polyester blanket with a picture of a leopard on it. I try to make it sound like no big deal, but I need to stress how important it is. "We just take a little tiny bit of fluid from an area far away from his spinal cord and then we send it off for tests. If he has an infection there that is untreated, he could get very sick. It could be serious…"

There are three adults in the room with this baby—Mom, Dad, and Uncle. Mom and Dad keep sighing and shaking their heads slowly while looking at the baby. They're really worried and not sure which is worse—whatever disease that's causing their baby to have a fever or whatever craziness this doctor wants to subject their baby to.

Uncle is on my side—he explains to me that they are all worried about the baby and then tells them that it is really important to know exactly what is going on so that we can take care of him in the right way. He looks at me and smiles. "Maybe we need a few minutes to talk this over and decide what to do."

"Muy bien," I say and head out to give them some space, hoping he'll convince them to go ahead with it.

I step outside and their nurse, Summer, asks me about what IV fluid to give the baby. "You ordered regular saline with dextrose but all we have is this diluted saline with dextrose—should I just give him that, then?"

She just graduated from nursing school. She's good and fun to work with and about my age. I want to make sure I'm not making her job any harder—that my orders are clear and make sense.

I see my attending, Pat, approaching. I head towards her while telling Summer, "Hmmm, well, you can just give him that diluted stuff, then. That should be OK."

Pat asks how I'm doing with the baby's family. Pat's tough and funny and just got through some kind of cancer treatment. Before it all happened they say she was really intense, harsh, and driven. After her diagnosis, she started eating all organic food and cut back on her formerly ridiculous work hours. She meditates, does yoga, goes to a naturopath, and has shiny acupressure beads taped to her ears that she squeezes every once in a while to deal with stress. Even with all that, her intensity comes through. "Hey, so are we going to do the spinal tap on that kiddo, like, yesterday?"

"Yeah, I think they'll consent, they're just talking it over now."

"Talking WHAT over? Go back in there and get them to do it—you don't fuck around with meningitis. If he has it, he needs to be treated right away or it could be bad, really bad. I saw your cutter guy and he's cool—you can get to him after we do that tap, and the ICU just picked up Mrs. Smith, so you have time."

I head back into the room and ask the family if they have any more questions.

"We'll do it," Uncle says. "But his mom wants to wait outside."

Summer and Pat and I set up and get ready. Summer helps Dad position the baby with his back curled up as much as possible. Unswaddled and pinned down, he starts screaming while I explain that the worst part of this for babies is that they don't like to be kept still like this. I'm not sure it's completely true, but one of my attendings said it once and it made me feel better. I clean off his back with cold Betadine and he cries harder. I find the landmarks I need to position the needle correctly while Pat hooks him up to a monitor and takes advantage of the Spanish-only family to tell me in English how sometimes kids can stop breathing during this procedure and how I should always have babies hooked up to monitors during spinal taps "just in case."

I put on sterile gloves and press the needle into his back. I'm doing my own version of prayer as I direct the needle through the spongy disc between the vertebrae. "Please, please, please let everything go well the first time—they're counting on me. I promised them. They trust me. Please, please, please."

I feel a pop as the needle pierces the tough layer protecting the spinal cord and sparkling clear fluid starts to drip out of the end of the needle. My whole body flushes with relief and I position the bottles under the drip, drip, drip and catch the fluid. It's so clear—it means that I had good technique and didn't hit a blood vessel. They call this a champagne tap.

I remove the needle, put a Band-Aid on the kid, and hand him back to his dad. I ask the clerk to rush the fluid down to the lab so we can get the results in about twenty minutes. Now that we have the fluid, we can start treating him with antibiotics, so I ask Summer to add the antibiotics right away—if he has meningitis, the sooner the better.

I take this time to call up the psychiatry resident and tell him about the wrist guy. He's impressed and says he'll be down within the hour. I pee, shove some food into my mouth, and sit down in the workroom to check the baby's lab results on the computer.

"Fifteen to twenty white blood cells in both tubes!" I announce this to Pat with a full mouth. The kid has meningitis—it could still be viral or it could be bacterial and we won't know for a few days while the cultures grow out. If it's bacterial it can be really bad but if it's viral it just gets better on its own without any treatment or complications. To be safe, you treat them with antibiotics in the hospital until you know for sure.

"OK!" She exclaims, raises her eyebrows, and clutches at her ear-beads. "OK. Did you get the antibiotics started already?"

I nod and swallow and grab the phone to call the pediatric resident. The resident answers my page and I start telling her the story.

"Yeah, so I've got a cute little two-month-old with a high fever and white cells in his spinal fluid."

"Yeah, OK—what's the scoop?"

I tell her the story, how the kid is otherwise healthy, what we did for him so far. "We started Amp and Gent and I gave him some fluid boluses…" I trail off.

"What's up?"

"I was just thinking about how I gave him dilute saline instead of regular. The nurse asked me what to use for maintenance and I told her just to do boluses with the same stuff. I guess that didn't do much good, huh. Probably didn't hurt him, though."

"Oooh, actually, giving tons of dilute fluid can dilute out their blood and then their brain can swell and all. I don't know how likely that is—I should look some stuff up and call my attending. I'll call you right back."

"OK." I hang up the phone; my stomach feels all floppy, like it's slithering down the inside of my body. My heartbeats are slamming in my head and I start breathing fast, my mouth gets dry. I realize that I may have completely fucked up here and now I'm going to have to deal with it. The fear is soon joined by shame. This is basic, foundation medical school stuff. It should be second nature by now.

My pager goes off again—it's the resident calling me back. I'm still sitting in front of the phone and realize that I've been staring at it for the past few moments—not moving.

"Hey, Amanda? Well, I read some case reports online just now and it turns out that we should probably get this kid to the intensive care unit so that he can be monitored. I'd also get some stat labs."

She tells me what to do, tells me that things will probably be fine, and that it could happen to anyone. "You'll never do that again, right? See, this is how we learn this stuff." It doesn't make me feel better. I hang up the phone and go find Pat, take a deep breath, and tell her what happened.

She says a few "Fucks" and then tells me it's not my fault, "it could happen to anyone." She calls the ICU attending to tell him what's headed his way. I tell Summer what happened. She says that it's all her fault, she swallows a couple of times and her eyes get shiny and she heads off to get ready to draw his blood. I go into the boy's room and try to explain to the parents that their son is going to be admitted to the hospital, that he has an infection in the fluid that bathes his brain, that he is going to a special place that can keep a really close eye on him because "we want to follow his labs, make sure he's OK."

They nod gravely, "Si, doctora."

I go sink into a work room chair and cry a little bit while Pat goes off with another resident to take care of a highway flag-woman who got run over by a truck.

Well, there's still the guy to sew up. While all of this other stuff has been happening the appropriate tools have been gathered at his bedside. I figure at least I can't mess this one up and maybe it's what I should end the night on. As I enter the room his 'sitter' looks up from her *People* magazine and reacts to my red puffy face. "Omigod, are you OK?"

"Things are *absolutely* just *perfectly* fine. Well let's *see* here, we have sutures we have all of the things we need, we are going to get you all fixed up in *no time flat!*" My voice is forced and perky cheerful.

The guy looks scared. "Are you OK? What's wrong?" His voice isn't flat anymore—he leans urgently towards me and looks at me, his pale eyes widening as he takes a deep breath. "What's going on, ma'am?"

"Nothing! There is nothing wrong whatsoever. Not a thing. Everything is just fine."

"Umm, well—I need to go to the bathroom."

"Sure, no *problem*! You and your sitter go to the bathroom and when we get back you'll be made as good as new!"

I left my pen in the baby's room, so I go and pick it up amongst the remnants of the spinal tap tray, the IV tubing, the crumpled sheet on the bed. Next to my pen is his little tiny newborn sock. Left behind. I pick it up and smell it—it smells like inexpensive detergent, and it's so unbelievably tiny, so perfectly white. I put it in the pocket of my lab coat and walk back to do the sewing.

On my way back I see that my patient is standing in the hallway talking to his nurse and his sitter, gesturing around him. He looks up at me as I walk by and they all turn to face me and stop talking. He looks down as I meet his gaze. His nurse walks toward me. "Hey, let's go talk over here," she says.

We go to the workroom and sit down. "Amanda, he doesn't want you to do the stitches—he says you look too upset and might not be able to do a good job."

"OK, let me get this straight. He slices his own arm because he can't deal with his emotions. I get a little upset and have the perfectly normal reaction of crying, and he doesn't want me to work on him because I might not be thinking clearly?"

We both start laughing.

"Fine. Fuck it. I'll go tell Pat."

Pat tells me to go to the cafeteria, get a real meal, and just chill.

Someone else gets to sew up the kid before he heads off to the psych ward. When I get back I look up the labs we drew on the baby every thirty seconds until the results show up in the computer—they're OK. Pat sends me home early and tells me to take the next night off. I go home and curl into bed, pick up the phone and call the peds ICU team. The kid is OK. He's stable and they're sending him to the regular floor for the rest of his meningitis observation period. I reach over to turn off the lamp, my hand resting briefly on the tiny white sock on my bedside table.

CUCUMBER CARS,

DRESS-UP CLOTHES,

AND A DOG NAMED BROCCOLI

Broccoli was a Homosexual

Maria Fabulosa

BROCCOLI WAS A HOMOSEXUAL. Not from the get go. He became one after the electrocution incident. Before then, he was a regular cocker spaniel, named after the floret-type curls that covered his long blond ears.

Broccoli was my dog, and even though he slept outside, he spent his afternoons with me in my room after I got home from grade school.

My parents had our house built right around the time I was born. With three kids and an infant, there were some details that never quite got finished. There were, for example, the live wires sticking right out of the wall in my room, underneath my desk.

"Stay away from those wires," my mom said when my brothers moved upstairs and the room became mine. "If you touch them, you'll get electrocuted."

"What's electrocuted?"

"Electrocuted is when you touch a live wire and your whole body becomes glued to the electricity until you are burnt to a crisp."

Wide-eyed silence.

"And it is very painful."

Wide-eyed nod.

"And it doesn't even happen quickly."

AFTER THAT LITTLE CHAT, I made sure the wires were hidden behind some sort of barrier; a pile of board games, a soccer ball…

I'm not sure what was covering the wires that day. All I know is that I was sitting at my desk, doing my homework. Broccoli was underfoot as always, sniffling around, fidgeting, scratching a flea off. All of the sudden I heard a blood curdling, high-pitched yelp. Then his body got real stiff by my feet. I quickly dropped to the floor to see what was happening. Broccoli was biting on the wires and getting electrocuted right in front of my eyes. There was a small puddle of pee on the hardwood floor beneath him.

I remembered my mom warning me: "Don't ever directly touch a person who's getting electrocuted." I grabbed the little play broom I had in my room and held it against his chest, trying to create a lever that would allow me to prod him off the wires. I pulled as hard as I could, screaming desperately, "Broccoli! Come on boy!" After a few seconds, he finally came off those wires and just plopped limply on the floor. By then my mom was standing at the doorway, "What happened, honey? Are you OK?"

"Broccoli bit the wires and got electrocuted." My heart pounded. No tears had managed to find their way out yet.

"Oh my God. Are you ok, honey?" She knelt next to me and hugged me tight.

"Is he dead, Mami?" Now I sobbed.

"I don't know, honey. Maybe."

I was holding his limp body close to me. All of the sudden I saw his eyeballs moving around, his nostrils flaring. "He's alive, Mami!" I cried from distress and relief.

He didn't get up right away, and when he did, he only managed to wobble over to his bowl and have a sip of water. After that he slept for three days.

I cleaned the little puddle of pee off the floor. The wood beneath the puddle was very dark brown, literally burned, as if acid had been spilled there.

After his recuperation, Broccoli developed some bizarre behaviors.

Fist of all, he developed a bloodthirsty hatred for my grandmother Rebeca. Every time she came around to our house, which was at least twice a week, he could sense her coming, and waited for her in ambush behind the gate. As soon as she opened it, he lunged for her ankle, biting hard and not letting go, somewhat reminiscent of the whole electrocution incident.

"Ay! Dios mio! Get this mutt off of me!" She screamed as she tried to kick him off with her free foot, always clad in a clunky black leather shoe.

But Broccoli never let go until she hobbled through the yard and stepped into the house. By that time, she always had a bloody ankle.

"Mari! Bring the rubbing alcohol and the Band-Aids for your grandmother."

"Si, Mami."

It was almost ritual. I never understood why my grandmother didn't call for someone to hold the dog before she stepped into the yard.

When my teenaged brother's friends walked through the yard, Broccoli lunged at their legs, too. But this was lust, not hatred. He waited for them in ambush, too, and when they stepped through the gate, he humped those boys' legs vigorously. "Get this mutt off my leg!" They'd yell, half embarrassed, half amused. Anything humping is always amusing to a fifteen-year-old boy. But Broccoli wouldn't let go until his love target stepped inside the house. He especially developed a deep love for the neighbor boy, Raul. When Raul came by, Broccoli humped him all the way inside the house. Sometimes he sat in our yard, looking longingly through the fence as Raul fixed his car across the street. Short cut-off jean shorts and flip-flops, his young chest smeared black with engine oil.

AFTER HIS ELECTROCUTION, Broccoli also got very fat. He became an obese blond homosexual cocker spaniel with his pansy curls. My dad was disgusted by this canine Liberace. "I'm going to find that faggot dog a bitch to breed with," he said one Sunday morning at the breakfast table, cleaning his thick square-framed glasses as he prepared to read the newspaper. "It must still be his instinct to want to breed with a bitch in heat."

A few days later he pulled up after work with the cutest little cocker spaniel princess in his car. He'd borrowed her from who-knows-who. My dad was a man of many friends, and if he decided he needed a dog in heat, he was sure to find one. She was young and slim, wore a sparkly pink collar.

Broccoli didn't flinch when he saw the dog, but she bee-lined for him, chasing him around the yard relentlessly. She was horny as hell and he was looking fine to her. My dad and I stood side by side, watching as Broccoli desperately tried to avoid this pushy bitch, looking for a place to hide. "I can't believe this!" My dad scratched his curly head, twitched his push broom mustache from left to right.

"Look dad, here comes Raul!"

When Raul walked through the gate, Broccoli ran towards him. It was just like one of those ending scenes from a romantic movie. The lovers running towards one another, hair flapping in the breeze. Only it was just

Broccoli running, and there was no breeze. He was so happy humping his beloved's leg! You could almost see a smile on his snout. Raul was humiliated, having to endure this lewd act as my dad watched, disgusted. And the poor princess, horny and dissatisfied, sat over at the corner of the yard, licking her inflamed rear end, unsure of what else to do with herself in such an awkward moment.

"This dog is a disgrace!" My dad said as he loaded the nice bitch in the blue Mitsubishi. "Who ever heard of a homosexual dog?!" Engine revving hard, "We ought to get rid of him."

"Yeah, get rid of him," said Raul as he finally shook Broccoli off his leg and walked inside the house.

Broccoli and I went inside also, shuffling our way down the hallway and into my room. I jumped from the doorway onto my bed. "Come on boy, up-up!" Broccoli managed a half-assed wag. Skirting around as far away from the wires as he could manage, he hopped onto the bed and curled into a fat ball next to me. "Don't worry, boy. Nobody's getting rid of you."

Turquoise Stilettos

Krystee Sidwell

THREE DAYS OF BEGGING has finally paid off. My mom has agreed to let me have the birthday party. My mom's best friends Jesse and Steve are in charge. They promise to make it unforgettable. I can't even believe I'm going to be living in Wyoming again, and just in time to turn thirteen. I wanted to spend my teenage years here in Vegas. Life totally sucks.

I'm going to invite like thirty people and Jesse talked my mom into letting us have wine coolers. First and foremost I have got to get a new outfit. Something sexy yet casual, so I can wear it this fall to eighth grade at the lame junior high in Casper.

I can't even believe I'm going to leave all of my friends in less than a week. I think leaving Micheline is going to kill me. I pray we visit each other all the time. I love being Vince's girlfriend. He's fifteen and a rapper on the radio. My life is so good I can't even believe that I have to leave and it's all because of my father. I hate him. Jesse and Steve are picking me up at three today so we can go to the mall. No mother. No mother bitching about appropriateness of the attire. No mother wanting to go to K-mart or the outlet stores. I am so excited I can barely stand it.

I notice as soon as they walk in the door that Jesse has a new perm and the top of his hair is really feathery. He also smells really good. Steve always has the same short bleached blonde spiked hair. I hope my hair looks cool at the party.

We walk into the mall through the food court. There are a hundred cute boys hanging out. I'm smiling at this cute skate punk when I hear Steve say to Jesse, "Don't you think it is time for miss thang's first pumps?" Then in unison I hear them screech the beautiful word: "Fredrick's!"

I can't believe my ears. I have been looking at the Fredrick's catalog secretly for like my whole life, and now they are taking me in there. I can feel the smile taking over my face. This is going to be the best shopping trip ever!

As we approach the front of the store my heart starts beating out of control. I feel a knot tightening around my guts. "Jesse, Steve, what if the lady figures out I'm not eighteen and kicks me out?"

"Oh sweet child, you don't have to be eighteen to be in there and besides that, dare anyone to tell you that you can't be somewhere we are, and we'll kick their asses. Now stand up straight and walk right in there like you own the goddamn place."

I did as I was told, and twenty minutes later we walked out the door with my first pair of stilettos. I love them. Micheline is never going to believe I got these bad-ass shoes! I hope I can learn to walk in them before the party. They are four inches high and really pointy and turquoise. I got black socks with lace around the ankles to wear with them.

Next we go into Contempo Casuals. This store is so cool. Madonna's *Holiday* is playing through the loudspeakers. I find what I want immediately! I can't believe how lucky I am! It's the most perfect outfit for my new shoes. We were looking for black because Steve says, "It's sexy for a woman to wear black to her birthday party, or any cocktail party for that matter." But, this is really the one. It's the same exact shade of turquoise as my shoes. A mini-skirt jumper with a three-inch wide elastic waistband. Jesse and Steve agree that this is the one. We get black fishnet stockings and big plastic turquoise hoops to create the entire ensemble.

For the finale of the day we get to buy makeup at the Saks' counter. This is like a dream come true. I will never forget these guys bringing me here. The lady helping me is so nice and beautiful. I totally hope I look like her when I'm old. She matches foundation and powder to my skin and shows me how to put it on so I don't stretch my skin into wrinkles.

I'm so tired after all that shopping. I hope my mother doesn't try to harass me about the shoes, makeup, or stockings.

IT'S THE DAY of my party. I'm so excited. I've been cleaning all morning and now I'm trying to lie down and take a nap so my skin is refreshed before the makeup and hair guys come over. Steve's friend, who does Joan Collins' makeup, is in town visiting and said he would come do my makeup. Sean is also coming over to do my hair. I hope I look so great. I wish I could have gotten Micheline a new outfit and makeup for my party, too. Oh well, she's way more pretty than me so she'll look good naturally.

As my friends start to arrive, Steve and Jesse let them in and greet the parents who are nervous that there isn't an adult chaperone. I'm still in the back getting my hair and makeup done. "You have to hurry, my friends are here."

"Your friends will wait for you to make an entrance."

"Um right, hurry!"

Twenty minutes later I am presented by Steve to the party. My hair is so cool. I have a really tall bang on one side that falls down over my eye and the other side is cut really short except one wisp by my ear. I am so happy. My friends are already drinking the wine coolers. My mom is out at the movie with her secret friend. A few guys are sliding into the pool down the slide like they're skateboarding, which really just makes them belly-flop when they get to the end. Things are getting really wild already. But where is my boyfriend?

As I approach the entry to look out the window, Vince walks in the front door. His eyes get so wide when he sees me. I do totally look so cool. For sure he'll never forget me now. "There you are. I've been waiting for you. Vince, are you alright? Quit staring at me."

"How can I? You are lookin' *fine*, cherry girl."

"Vince, want to kiss me tonight?"

"Cherry, I want to do more than that. Now you're going to move away and look at you! You are too fine. How can I let you leave, and in a year or two give it up to some white cowboy hick? You have to beg your mom to stay. Maybe my mom or Micheline's mom will let you live here with us."

"First, no way is my mom letting me stay here. Second, no mom around here needs extra kids. Third, I haven't done it with you—you I adore—how do you think I'll be able to do it with any Wyoming guys? Get real. Now, are we going to kiss tonight?"

"Sure I'm going to kiss you. Where should we?"

"In the laundry room."

"OK. You go in first, then I'll come in a few minutes later, that way no one will notice."

I go into the laundry room and sit down on top of the washer while I wait. I am sweaty. My heart feels just like it did days ago when I bought these great shoes. Pounding, Pounding, Pounding. This is a worse kinda pounding. I feel like I could puke any minute now. Vince walks in and softly closes the door behind him. "Are you sure you're ready for our first big kiss, my cherry? I don't want you to feel rushed just because you are moving."

"Yes, Vince, it's a kiss. Come on, I can't get pregnant or AIDS from a kiss, you know?"

He steps up to me. I can feel the door of the washer dent a little under my weight. I hope it doesn't make a loud popping noise. He pushes his body in between my knees, pulls me forward and says, "OK, Cherry, here we go."

I lean down and our lips touch. He spreads mine open with his tongue and he tastes musty and warm. It's pretty weird that his tongue is in my mouth but I think I really like it. I put my tongue in his mouth and we just keep moving our tongues around for a really long time.

"So what did you think?"

"I think it's good. I like the way your lips feel really fluffy and strong."

"I'm really glad we kissed. I won't ever forget you."

I step out of the laundry room and back out into the party. Steve catches my eye and winks a knowing wink. I think it's time to swim, so I change into my swimsuit and dive in.

Lessons in Blue Velvet

Kelli Grinich

MY OLDEST AND DEAREST FRIEND, Susie, was getting married. Hardly the image of the blushing bride, Susie was forty-two and her crows-feet lined eyes were puffy and exhausted from morning sickness. Her Vera Wang wedding dress was being let out to accommodate her four-month pregnant body. My bridesmaid dress had been painstakingly taken in at the bust by a professional tailor who knew how to work with velvet.

Oh, who am I kidding? It was a size eighteen dress, and damn it, I 'd never bought a size-eighteen anything. Of course the chest was huge and needed to be adjusted. The rest fit just fine. Well, sort of.

I squeezed into the fragile, soft gown and turned to let Susie button me.

"Elegant. You'll wear it again," Susie crooned as she nibbled on soda crackers.

The dress was full length—nearly six feet of inky blue velvet. The slit up the back alone was high enough to let an army of dwarfs march through. Thirty covered buttons climbed up my back from my waist to the high velvet covered neck—but not before disappearing into the sheerest blue fabric that clung as tight as skin to my spine and shoulder blades. The sheer, second-skin fabric traveled down each arm to the velvet-trimmed wrist. When I closed my eyes, I felt warm and completely encased in fabric. Which just proves that illusion is everything. When I turned and looked at myself in the mirror, I saw the most naked, whorish dress I could ever imagine wearing in public. The dress was so tight that you could make out an impression of my pubic hair even through the velvet nap. The sheer bodice fabric stretched over the shoulders and down my chest to just above my nipples, then boldly trailed between my breasts toward my belly to the point where the top of my striped Jockey panty band was showing. My bigger breast, half covered in velvet, half in sheer, created a huge diagonal wrinkle in the cleavage of canyon between boobs.

Yikes. This was going to take major underwear. I looked around at the other four bridesmaids. We all looked like aging hookers in various stages of sag and bulge.

SUSIE MET PAUL through a personal ad on the Internet. Dating in Chicago had been hard on Susie. Twenty years of partners, of princes and toads, had jaded most of our group of five bridesmaids. This was the farthest that she had taken a relationship, and we wondered what her future would hold. If Susie's love life was a three-layer cake, it would be sprinkled with a multitude of names and experiences. In 1989 alone, her heart was shattered by a city councilman who was scandalously unfaithful and then, four months later, re-broken by a dark-eyed Italian plumber who wrecked her car and pocketed her jewelry. Fortunately, this thin layer of dense bittersweet experience became a strong foundation that supported Susie's next eight years of dating. High and broad, the middle layer was dressed with a goo that enshrined the souls of the guys most of us had never met. Susie loved men of all ages, colors, hair thicknesses, and marital statuses. The one thing that most of the men had in common were the words "This is The One" branded on them. Some men had lasted a week, some men a year, and several wove their way in and out of her life for decades.

And then came Paul. Fresh from the shower, fresh from the Internet. Fresh, tall, and wealthy. Paul was not just employed, he was a home owner. Finally, here was the top layer, frosted in butter-cream and bliss. When the engagement was announced, I was on the first plane from Austin. The couple wanted to marry right away, and Susie wanted to shop for wedding dresses. As she whisked me away from the airport into the city, she chatted about her job, her family, and her first impression of Paul.

"He acts gay," she said. "He had a natty blue blazer on, and his voice was kind of high when we first met, and sort of affected. Of course, he's NOT gay, but that was my first impression. Lots of different men sit down to pee, and besides, he mountain bikes and wants to have children right now," she chirped.

My ears perked up in alarm. Gay?

SIX MONTHS HAD GONE BY and now the nuptials were nearly upon us. Sickened by the fact that I looked like Cher's great-aunt trying on her Vegas outfits, I headed to Nordstrom to beg for a miracle in the lingerie department. My hopes were hanging on the assumption that this was the one department store that sized spandex as well as they do shoes. The saleswoman looked pleasant, even eager to help me. I started out by stating that I needed a strapless bra and black hose that were low cut but that wouldn't result in panty lines, stuttering something about blue velvet and sheer netting. As I spoke, I started losing nerve, realizing that what I really needed was to lose thirty pounds. My saleswoman, expertly trained in the rules of intimate undergarment warfare, quickly swept me into a dressing room. Thirty minutes later, my skin rubbed pink from trying on elastic banding and under-wires, I stood in the perfect under-armor for the bridesmaid dress. The miracle was called a bustier-panty underslip.

The bustier bone inserts pushed my breasts into mounds Picasso would have been proud of. Secret pockets in the black lace held bits of fluff that created a symmetrical landscape on either side of the bare, belly-diving plunge. Gravity was both honored and defied in the process. Perhaps the crowning achievement happened when the saleswomen handed me the black, thigh-high stockings. In combination with the one-piece-bike-short-bustier contraption, the result was a smooth silhouette from chest to toe. From the mirror, my middle-aged, mother-of-three-body was reminiscent of the body I'd known in the mid 1980s.

Looking back on the wedding day, would it matter that my lingerie cost three times that of the bridesmaid dress? Absolutely not. It mattered that I looked and felt my best as my dear friend approached the riskiest decision of her life—to marry someone that she hadn't declared the "One." Slowly we started the step-tap, step-tap down the aisle toward the altar. The bridesmaids had determined to walk the traditional march just minutes before the wedding when we realized that any broader stride might result in a "Climb and Separate" phenomena with the back slit of the velvet dress. I was thankful for the arm of Glenn, my groomsman. While he was not nearly tall enough and had forgotten his socks, Glenn seemed certainly the least drunk of the five groomsmen.

As we proceeded forward through the cathedral, Glenn walked his own version of step-tap and pulled me slightly closer. Looking up at me with gin eyes and a surprisingly steady gaze, Glenn whispered in my ear: "Nice hooters."

I grinned. Maybe I would wear the dress again.

My Sister, Defiant Bride

Mira Shah

WEDDINGS GIVE ME A RASH. The dress, the flowers, the emotion, the ritual. When I was six, I told my father, Arun Shah, I was never going to get married. He laughed, wrote it down on a piece of paper, dated it, and put it in his wallet. Smugly, he thought he'd pull it out when I came home years later to share the news of my engagement. It was never to be so. Instead, I came home fourteen years later to introduce my girlfriend.

On my parents' thirty-fifth wedding anniversary, my sister Mina announced her engagement. Thank God, I thought. My parents, who seemed somewhat bored in their retired years, would finally have a project to focus on and could celebrate someone who followed in their path. They called me up, 3,000 miles and three time zones away, to tell me the Big News.

"Congratulations!" I said with genuine enthusiasm.

Mina deserved happiness in her life. She was sandwiched between me and my youngest sister, Maya, who came along when Mina and I were school age. She was quietly effective in a house where strong personalities ruled. As the middle child, she was granted the privilege of mediating all conflict between my mother and I and, in return, I stole her clothing, bossed her around, and never once came to her social rescue when the snotty girls at St. Francis of Assisi Elementary School found her to be a good moving target. Now, at twenty-eight, she'd found her niche in Charlotte, North Carolina as an environmental health specialist. She would marry Mark Brookes, forest analyst and avid Ohio State fan.

As I cheered for the newly engaged couple from the opposite coast, Mina told me that she wanted a simple wedding, probably in the mountains, with close friends and family. Nothing elaborate.

Then the nightmare began.

MINA'S SIMPLE WEDDING PLANS turned out to be very specific. Unfortunately, my mother and father—individually—had their own detailed wedding fantasies. None of their ideas seemed to intersect. I guess it shouldn't have been a surprise. We're talking about three very different people. My father, a first generation immigrant from Mumbai, landed in the states for his post-secondary education, where he met my white Irish Catholic mother. He broke an eight-year arranged marriage agreement and embraced the American way of life. My mother, one of ten children born to fiery parents who'd coined the phrase "do it now or I'll rip your arm off and beat you with the bloody stump," is the polar opposite of an aspiring Indian bride. Mina, the product of the most unlikely cultural match since Tex-Mex, would use her wedding plans as an opportunity to individuate.

Typically, I was the one who bore the brunt of my parents' natural tendency micromanage milestones. I know my sisters were jealous that my father archived my entire college orientation on video. And I'm sure they feel I received much better driving instruction from my mother who clutched the passenger door handle on our inaugural trip to the grocery store involuntarily yelling "Stay away from the mailboxes! Stay away from the mailboxes!" As the oldest child, my parents seemed to experience many of my milestones as their own, and now as Mina took the adult milestone lead, I wondered if she knew what she was in for.

And I had no idea I was trading ritual abuse for a new job: mediator.

My mother took an active role in the wedding planning process—she visited venues and went to bridal fairs and had many, many opinions.

But Mina was not interested in my mother's ideas. "I've been ignored for years, and now mom wants to hone in on the most important day of my life," she said.

"Just give her a few jobs. She'll be happy," I said, trying to quell my sister's frustration. And that she did, outlined in an e-mail that was also routed to me. A line in the sand had been drawn. Phrases like "you will" and "you never" jumped off the computer screen. Emboldened sentences like, "I need you to respect my boundaries," read like "back off bitch," and were branded forever in e-mail. I stared at the computer screen in horror, 3,000 miles from the battlefield.

"I just don't understand why she treats me this way," my mother cried on the phone. "We're trying to give her everything she wants. Aren't mothers supposed to be involved?"

"Yeah, ah, I don't know where she's coming from," I said, trying to sound neutral.

It didn't last long.

Then my father asserted his wedding need. He wanted to bring his family over from India for the wedding. My mother and my sister were finally on the same side: "Absolutely Not!"

My sister threw a fit. "They can come, but don't expect me to entertain them," she told me indignantly. "If they come, Dad is going to spend all his time attending to their needs. I need him to do things for me."

"Dad doesn't really ask for much," I tried. I thought that the individual paying for the $15,000 wedding should have an opportunity to choose some of the wedding guests.

But the cultural rift between our family and our Hindi relatives was long and deep. My mother had attempted to reside in Mumbai after my parents married. When she stepped off the plane, her welcoming gift was a list of names. She was encouraged to choose one. Because my father had broken his arranged marriage promise and married an American, my grandparents made a quick social move to ensure that the neighborhood would not immediately know that my father had married a western woman. Hypothetically, Sheila, the chosen name, would cloak my mother's blonde hair, blue eyes, and fair skin that turned bright red when hit by the intense Indian sun. My parents lasted about a year before returning the States.

In my young life, I'd visited India twice, once as a ten-year-old tomboy and again as a twenty-two-year-old feminist. For our family, it was like National Lampoon's Vacation goes to Mumbai. "Why do you wear gentlemen's clothing?" many of them asked me repeatedly. "Why do you live in another town away from your parents?" and "Why do each of you have your own car?" They were perplexed by our void of Indian culture, tradition, and identity.

I explained all these elements to an old friend who picked me up at the Atlanta airport and headed me down to my family's suburban home in Macon, Georgia. As we drove down I-75, passing sprawling development and commerce, I described my mother's yearning to actively bond with my sister through the wedding process and instead ending up with a prescription for Zoloft. I told of my sister's boundary-drawing e-mails and of her feelings that nothing was going her way. I barely had time to describe the added element of Indian relatives who were likely to be appalled by the Western wedding. "My sister, defiant bride," I said as we passed a huge sign for the Bible Factory Outlet. "It's like Bridezilla on bovine growth hormone."

I'd flown into Atlanta hoping to spend a few days with friends who might ground me for the part-Southern, part-Buckeye, Indian-infused wedding. However, I was instructed to come to Macon as quickly as possible. My dad's younger brother, who had also immigrated to the States, had planned to be in charge of the visiting Hindus; however, while sprucing up his apartment for their arrival, he fell and broke his shoulder. Now it was up to me to play recreational director and help drive them to the wedding site nearly six hours away. "So you want me to come two hours south and then drive six hours north with how many people in the car?" I asked. My inner tantrum-throwing seven-year-old was about to emerge.

When we pulled up to my parents' home, the front yard was already awash with family members who hadn't seen me in ten years. My hair was now shorter than most males my age. My partner, twelve years my senior and with two sons, eighteen and twenty-two, would be coming to join us later in the week. When I asked my mother if any of our relatives knew I was gay, she said, "I've left that up to your father." That meant that they did not yet know. When my partner, Wendy, asked, "will anyone at this wedding know that we're a couple?" my only reply was "everyone except the three people in Indian dress." I thought it would be handy for her to have a visual reminder.

Surely the Indian relatives would be gracious to Wendy. After all, they'd assume that she was my housemate, a poor forty-four-year-old divorcee who'd traveled from Oregon because, obviously, she was being shunned by society. I couldn't even attempt to think about explaining Wendy's role in my life. Right now, I had bigger fish to fry.

"You are so skinny."

"Your hairs are so short."

"You are too skinny."

The comments came from all directions.

"You need to eat something."

I watched as my friend waved and drove off back toward I-75, the last vestige of my reality to be seen for days. I took a deep breath and walked toward the house, cursing my sister's bridal name every step of the way.

The days preceding the wedding went smoothly, as long as I did as I was told. Much of the time I was told to eat and handed a plate of Indian food. One day, after the fifth plate of curried vegetables, paneer, and chapatti, I dumped some spicy fried Indian snacks in the woods behind the house.

"I saw what you did with food," my uncle shouted when I came back in the house. "How are you ever going to get Indian husband if you don't eat Indian food? You need to grow your hairs."

The bride was in North Carolina, far from the excessive eating and concern for my matrimony. I'd called her from the airport and informed her that I had folded my bridesmaid's dress and placed it delicately in my backpack. "Will there be a place to iron it?" Silence. I decided to change the subject.

The wedding would be in the mountains outside Asheville. Originally, the location seemed ideal—close enough to a liberal pocket to escape the confines of family—but upon arriving at our destination, Lake Lure, the famed film locations for both *Dirty Dancing* and *The Last of the Mohicans*, I noticed some of the local color. Confederate flags flew from the awnings of many shops in the town, and one shop specialized in lacquered knotty pine plaques with sayings like, "I like my women like I like my guns, LOADED."

Was Mina trying to make sure that we were all killed before the actual wedding? Had she lost her mind? Had she forgotten every vacation we ever took as a family during which my mother would not let any of us get out of the car in towns just like this? Had she forgotten that even though we lived in a white world, we really didn't look white?

The Indians seemed intrigued with the mountain charm. "When we get to the house we have an outfit for you to put on, OK?" my aunt winked.

Oh, good God. A favorite pastime of my Indian relatives and real way to connect culturally was to allow them to dress me in full Hindi regalia. Sari, bindi, and jewelry. After I was fully adorned, several photos of me with every familial combination possible would be taken—Indian me and my parents; Indian me, my aunt, and cousin; Indian me with my uncles and dad; Indian me with everyone. It was if I was a life-size cut-out of Elvis himself.

When Mina finally arrived in the gated mountain community of Lake Lure, she seemed relatively unimpressed with the journey we had survived through three southern states in a Honda Odyssey full of East Indians.

"We didn't even get asked once if we were related to Osama Bin Laden, not even in the Wendy's in Clemson, South Carolina," I told her, but she was immune to our struggle.

Mina made an interesting housing choice for all of us. The house, which was actually quite nice, had a hot tub, two bedrooms, an open loft, and a couch with a pullout bed. If you were heterosexual, married, or about to be married, you were granted a room with a door. If you were gay or heterosexual and living with your boyfriend—like my youngest sister— or heterosexual and not yet arranged to be married—like my Indian cousin,

Rupal—you got the open loft. And, if you were fifty, never married, never mentioned a sexual preference, and had a broken shoulder, then you got the couch; but don't expect anyone to pull it out for you.

Two days before the wedding, Wendy finally arrived. She flew to the Asheville/Hendersonville Regional Airport and I was relieved to go pick her up. Unfortunately, with no signage or ambient light in the mountains of North Carolina, I went forty miles in the wrong direction. By the time I found Wendy sitting in a rocking chair on the makeshift porch of the Regional Airport, I was distraught.

"And then my uncle yelled at me about some food and he keeps telling me I will never find an Indian husband, and then they dressed me up." I couldn't stop recounting the previous days' violations. "We're not going back to that house tonight." I left the parking lot and pulled into the Best Western.

"Oh, you're not kidding," Wendy said.

We managed to find a six-pack of beer and when we asked where we could find a bottle opener, we were directed to Super Wal-Mart.

Wendy, an Australian and a professional beer opener, took control. With a flick of the wrist and a door jam, the libations were flowing. Finally, we were happily lounging on the bed and watching cable TV with the romantic hum of the air conditioner in the background.

The next morning we found the lesbian coffee house. For a brief moment, I forgot how many different ways I was going to ruin my sister after this was over. We inquired where we could find some nearby cosmetics, a necessity for any bridesmaid. "Are we near a mall?" I asked.

"Well, we do have Wal-Mart," said the cute woman with square glasses, short hair, and a "George Bush Out of my Uterus" T-shirt as she handed me my coffee.

Why was everyone trying to send us to Wal-Mart?

THE BIG DAY ARRIVED. By this time I was exhausted from playing cultural ambassador, acting like a dress-up doll, and admiring a framed pencil sketch of a church, fine artwork from the Buckeye State proudly presented to my Hindu father by the Brookes family as a gift of unity.

My dress survived its folded state and I stood with my sister and other bridesmaids for photos at the gazebo on the lake. My sister had been relatively calm, but when she saw all the speedboats on the lake nearby, she started yelling, "Get out of here," at the top of her voice. She'd been told that part of the lake would be off limits around wedding time. She yelled again over the buzz of motors and music cruising the lake. The happy boaters hollered and waved in excitement at the bride. She was not impressed. "Get out of here," she shouted. She was starting to look a little crazy.

"Mina, shut up! Do you realize that any one of those boaters may have a gun? Do you realize where we are?" The words flew out of my mouth.

She stared at me in horror. "Don't tell me to shut up on my wedding day." Her eyes burned through my skin like bug repellent.

There was no winning this game.

The wedding ceremony took place with boats floating in the Lake Lure backdrop. One tourist cruise parked and waited for the groom to kiss the bride. I sunk into resignation about my place in history as the minister highlighted the perks of being legally bound to someone for eternity. Even though it was easy to hear the minister's assertive voice, she was completely obscured by the bride and groom, who towered over her four-foot-nine-inch stature. It seemed like wedding by teleconference. The Indians, excited at the onset of the ceremony, were perplexed by its brevity; a typical Hindi wedding lasts several days.

At the reception, I did my best to keep my dad and his brothers on beat to the music. It was easiest if I put them in a row. Then Mark's mother made a spectacular gift presentation for the bride and groom. She sparkled in her slinky iridescent ensemble as she highlighted Mark's proud Kentucky heritage and pulled out a jar of real Kentucky moonshine. Mark unscrewed the top and took a sip. He balked at the vile taste of his ancestors. Mina took the bottle, threw back her head, and swilled the pure grain alcohol.

The Cucumber Car

Lainie Keslin Ettinger

THROUGH THE FRENETIC SWIRL of toddler bodies pushing toy shopping carts, slithering into miniature houses, and hoarding plastic produce, my eighteen-month-old daughter Maddie spied her destination. With a lethal combination of determination and legs that had only recently progressed from lurching in small, jerking steps to running in wobbly unpredictable strides, she took off.

My husband and I watched her with varying degrees of pride and concern. This was not our first visit to the fast-paced miniature metropolis of our local science museum. It was like stepping into Willie Wonka's Chocolate Factory with an array of colors, moving parts, and Baby Gap-clad oompa loompahs bouncing off the walls. It was survival of the fittest in this place.

My husband, Steve, was unfazed by the over-stimulating environment; he was a veteran. He knew how to guide Maddie through the chaos without controlling her. Maddie had a history of dashing into the water station first, pouring buckets of water over her head, and then rolling in the sandbox, coating herself like a breaded cutlet. Steve could effortlessly guide her toward the safety of the flubber table and keep her from submerging herself at the water table until the end of the visit. He was also a master of quick, efficient diaper changes in the field. He calmly attacked gruesome diaper explosions in the most primitive surroundings like a skilled army surgeon. While I worried constantly about bringing sufficient rations of snacks, bottles, and changes of clothes, there seemed to be only one thing that elevated Steve's anxiety level: other children. He was convinced that through either accident or design, the other babies and toddlers were determined to knock Maddie down, contaminate her with their runny noses, or inflict bodily harm. He flanked her like a presidential secret service agent with his arm held out to keep the throngs of ill-mannered, unwashed, contagious varmints away from his kid.

From the safety of the mini-grocery store check-out line, I watched the scene unfold like slow-motion footage of an intricate football play. Maddie made a tipsy dash for the coveted cucumber car, a four-foot-long, stationary vehicle made of wood and Plexiglas. This was a slick ride, and every kid in the place knew it. Steve lunged in from the side, swooping in to do the advance work before Maddie reached the car. I watched him closely to make sure he didn't elbow any three-year-olds out of the way. Instead, he bent down to clear out stray pieces of synthetic food that had migrated from the bilingual grocery store/Mercado area and were stashed inside the car.

As Steve removed the plastic food, he suddenly stopped cold. After grabbing what he thought was a plastic potato, he stood up with his arm outstretched. For the first time ever, I saw his face contort in fear. He let out a series of pained screams, "Aaahh! Aaahh! Aaahh!" just like the guy in *The Godfather* who wakes up to find a horse's head in his bed. In the palm of Steve's hand was a perfectly formed, fresh log of poop. Some child—someone *else's* child—had mistaken the cucumber car for the potty car. Steve was traumatized. "It's still warm!" he said in disgust as he dropped the offending brown lump back into the cucumber car. We called over a volunteer who summoned the museum's haz-mat squad to tape-off and sanitize the area. In a daze, Steve rushed off to the bathroom to wash his hands. He returned twenty minutes later, still shaken by the experience and told me, "I just can't wash my hands enough. They'll never feel clean again." Steve learned what mothers of small children have always known but never say out loud: Cleaning up the poop of someone else's child is disgusting. Tending to your own kid's poop is just part of the job.

The years passed, and we returned to the museum many times with both Maddie and then our younger daughter. I took savage delight in encouraging them to, "take Daddy for a ride in the cucumber car."

Long after our run-in with the cucumber car, I got a job at the museum and discovered that the little hotrod was to be decommissioned. I relentlessly e-mailed and called the exhibits manager. Finally, after six months, he told me that I could have the cucumber car. A friend with a roomy SUV agreed to help me transport my prize as long as I let her disinfect it with bleach spray first. I agreed, but I reminded her that over one million children had played in the cucumber car since Steve's horrific discovery. Surely it had been cleaned since then. We brought the cucumber car to my house and placed it in the center of the living room. I was giddy, waiting for Steve to come home at the end of the day. When he finally opened the door, he saw his old nemesis.

It was the best Father's Day present I ever gave him.

HOW TO LEAVE A PLACE

Just Go

Amy Lee

THE FIRST TIME is easy. You've got no choice. Just go. What's left? If you fight, you'll lose. You used to fight when you had no choice. You lost every time. Home was a mood mine, each glance a step, each step a risk like every unchecked word. If you stay, you will die. So how can you stay? You're still too young to see that zombies actually manage quite well. So you run to avoid death. You run for your life!

You are teen-powered hope and righteousness, trying to outrun death. Soon you will notice that you're growing zombie skin. But first, a job for food and friends, a place to belong. A new place. A place to start all over. Walgreens, Sugar Land, Texas. Four suburban bucks an hour graveyard shifts. Something about working graveyard stirs you. You wear poetic lenses. The unrelenting buzzing lights. A chance for freedom that forgets the way it was before. This is graveyard after all, eternal meager night.

You meet Gwen, and you're in love with her gold front tooth. There's a martini glass etched into it. She's brown, like you, and hates her job as much as you pretend it's cool. She tells stories about her church and shows you pictures of her grandkids—way too young to have any. You wonder if you really care, can't hide that you do. Gwen warms up those wee hours, makes the checklist of slavish duties seem like poetry. Something impossible, but look beyond. You both wear teal vests with big pockets, and Gwen shows you how to steal candy by taking it to the stock room first. You eat so much candy back there. Then you think to use Gwen's trick for smokes, but you can't tell her. That's going too far. She goes to church, after all.

Mr. Voradakis has garlic breath and a wolfish smirk. He's called mister because he signs the checklist and counts the till. And because his vest is grey, not teal like yours and Gwen's. You catch him watching you sideways a lot and worry that it's about the cigarettes. You're too young to know that zombies tend to watch their prey sideways. He always talks so close. That's how you know his breath, like humid garlic sweat. He's not supposed to be letting you work graveyard because you're too young. You owe him for letting you. You're in a bind, remember? He warns you not to tell about his favor. You might get him in trouble, and you'll never see Gwen again. It starts reminding you of home, like a grave.

But this time there's a choice. You choose to go. It's much harder this way. You choose to leave Gwen, throw that ugly teal vest on the ground. You choose again. You're still too young to see that this again won't be the last, again and again. But you're starting to get how zombies work. They count the till and smell rotten. The last shift you work, you take a whole carton. Gwen gives you a ride in her faded blue Astro Van. You've never been with Gwen outside the store before. A strange new freedom. You want to tell her about the carton burning in your bag, but she's talking about her church again. She wants you to go with her sometime. She prays for you. You wonder if zombies go to church. You're pretty sure zombies wouldn't think to run, and so you must.

Growth and Management Techniques

Margaret McConnell

THE INTERCOM FLASHES as I unload maps, a camera, and muddied paperwork onto my desk. It's been a long day's journey driving and hiking. *Buzz, buzz.* A voice follows.

"Can I see you in my office?"

"Be right up."

The windows of the building are steamy. I take off my wool sweater, dust off forest debris, and climb the stairs, looking out over dramatic architecture. Clearly, the team who created this organization held lofty ideas—the space reflects it. A soaring ceiling and full glass façade reveal views of the surrounding state park. Modular work stations dot the floor, each with a flag overhead. My desk sits at the center, behind a large bronze hand holding a fragile glass replica of our planet.

It's a world forestry group, created in the eco-friendly seventies, intended to be a progressive think-tank and haven. Interns come from abroad to study American growth and management techniques, then leave behind papers outlining their own. I'm the new Program Manager, just ten weeks into the job. The founders were striving for conservation, but it seems the team today is more focused on forest *products*—and profit.

Confusing. Especially in my first "not-for-profit" experience.

And that's not the only source of confusion.

I'VE BEEN WORKING for decades, but I've traveled, too. References to trips abroad pepper my resume and attempt to excuse the gaps in my work history. For the first time, those gaps have helped land me a job. It's been a bumpy start, but I'm optimistic. The organization hasn't been thriving in recent years—twenty desks, twenty flags, three interns. Sometimes I think it's good we're such a small group, coexistence is an already-delicate operation.

Kelly's from Australia: Well-muscled basketball player and highly opinionated. Worked as a pharmacist in her twenties, returned to school in her thirties. Now she's a tree doctor. She's traveled the world between jobs and college semesters. I relate to her life-choices, but not her worldview. "I found a cricket club here, thought of joining," she tells me. "Went for a look-see, but, (here she lowers her voice) *mostly sub-continent players.*" She curls her top lip, waves her hand in a "shoo-fly" kind of way, "No thanks. I'll stick to basketball at the Y."

Enrique's from Chile: Young, in love, and notably quiet. Signed up for a math course at the community college and met an American girl. They plan to marry in a year but I wonder what they talk about. Each day I greet him with limited results. "Hi Enrique! How are you today?" I ask. He holds up a steady hand, then returns to his studies. I assume it's a cautious wave, not a "please come no further" warning, but it's hard to be sure.

Fernando's from Brazil: Tall, middle-aged. Impossibly gracious and simultaneously demanding. Financed the internship with his own scarce resources and hopes to find a better job when he returns home. His wife, six-year-old daughter, and newborn baby get by on their own in the meantime. He calls them often, then fills me in on daily family life. He approached me a few weeks ago and bowed in greeting, "Hello Margaret. I am speaking to my daughter today and she is very much wanting a Tinky Winky doll. I am hoping I will be able to do this for her very soon."

"Yes, Tinky Winky!" I'd been hearing this news for weeks, wondered why he kept mentioning it. Then, slowly, it dawned on me—*I* was supposed to get the Tinky-Winky.

I assume I seem funny in ways I have no ability to see. My boss has expressed it directly. I fit a stereotype of some kind—California liberal—soft, idealistic.

But I'm not soft. I'm firm. And it throws them off.

I REACH THE TOP of the stairs, approach the office door. A stained-oak nameplate reads "Clara Li, Director." I knock to announce myself, then walk in.

"Hi, Clara. How are you?"

"Fine, thank you. How was the trip today?" She stands formally in front of her desk wearing a tailored pale green polyester suit. She's five feet tall with plain features. Her hair is black, short, and frizzy. She has a twin sister who's quite beautiful, and Clara jokes that she herself is just an old man, thinly disguised as a young woman.

"It was good. We visited two mills, and one test farm. Found our way 'round pretty well, made some contacts, and the interns asked good questions."

Clara gestures to the small meeting table where a lone white envelope rests at the center. "Can you take a seat please?"

CLARA WAS BORN in Taiwan, but raised in Singapore. She lives with her mother and sister in a stately home. It's a banking family—like, the *owners* of the bank. She tells colorful stories of her father coming to visit with suitcases of money, and her grandfather in Taiwan, who claims he and friends will fight to the death armed from rooftops if their freedom is compromised. And she tells me that it's bad I'm a Dragon woman. Kelly, too.

"Dragon women? Two? Oh, that's very bad. The power of the Dragon takes a man far in life, but it makes a woman too difficult. It can only destroy her."

Each day, the group eats lunch together at Clara's request, and she holds court over the proceedings as we sit around a folding table in our small kitchen. I've usually reheated rice and curry from dinner out the previous night. Clara's lunch will be similar, but homemade.

"Jackie Chan has a new movie," she'll say, pulling Saran Wrap off her porcelain bowl. "I recommend it—karate like ballet. Martial art performed as dance. Extraordinary."

It's a common start to the lunch hour, Clara reviewing movies or restaurants. With time, I realized she was paraphrasing the morning paper. She follows this with political or social commentary, which does not share the same origin.

"Of course I'm not a fan of the Chinese. We Taiwanese are a different people. They say the only thing straight, you know, *honest*, about the Chinese is the hair."

Kelly may have her own racial biases, but reserves them for private conversation; OK to hold the prejudice, bad taste to express it in a mixed group. As I look down the table, I notice her frowning in open frustration, her sandwich suspended over a Tupperware container.

Enrique sits quietly, twisting noodles on a fork.

Fernando stirs, then rests his fork on the table. "Kelly, do you make the sandwich for dinner, too?"

She laughs, spitting out the tiniest piece of turkey. I've heard her boast of how well she eats. "I usually have steak for evening tea, sometimes chicken, steam up some veg. Sandwiches are *a mid-day meal*," she instructs, mouthing the words slowly.

Enrique and Fernando exchange a look.

"What do you guys do for dinner?" I ask.

"Top Ramen," they say in unison. They bring it everyday for lunch, too.

Clara turns in surprise, "You're eating dehydrated noodles day and night?"

Fernando nods. "We don't know cooking."

Enrique's voice is gentle. "My fiancé cannot come to the apartment before the wedding. Her father's rule. But I eat at the family home on weekends."

"My mother may come to help," Fernando adds. "We are seeing about the airfare."

"What? All the way from Brazil?" Clara is incredulous. "There's got to be a simpler solution."

I don't think it's my imagination. Three sets of eyes turn to me.

A WEEK EARLIER, Clara had confronted me about Tinky Winky. She said Fernando needed my help and that I should do the shopping for him. I remembered his happy tales of buying furniture in town and wondered why toy shopping might be different.

Not wanting the task, and not wanting trouble, I tried to find a middle ground. I called the department store across from his apartment, confirmed they had the toy in stock, wrote down the price, the hours, etc., and gave Fernando the information.

It worked. The next day he presented me with the purple doll.

"Thank you, Margaret. Now it must be a gift, with the special paper, and then it goes in the mail." He pushed it toward me.

I gently pushed it back, then looked up, and he was gone. Clara stood staring from across the room.

I *wanted* to be working on tasks in my job description: creating a code system for our library, researching new data for the U.S. forestry report, planning the two-week industry tour we'd take in the summer, arranging for Japanese visitors. But I spent my day as a diplomat instead, arranging a safe international journey for Tinky Winky. I shopped for the necessities, wrapped the gift nicely in kid-friendly paper, added a big purple bow. Then I packed it safely in a brown box and headed off to the post office.

I did, after all, want to keep the peace.

AFTER THE TOP RAMEN conversation, I told Clara, "I can entertain the staff at my apartment once or twice this year, and arrange a few Friday night dinners downtown, but please don't ask me to cook for the male staff." I laughed, hoping it wasn't even a possibility in her mind.

"You *could* do more to help the interns," was all she said.

CLARA AND I sit across from each other at the small meeting table.

"Margaret, this was a difficult decision, and I'm sorry to do this now, after an especially long day, but I'm letting you go. This is your final check." She nudges it in my direction.

I sit and wait. I expect more information… an explanation. But she says nothing.

I'm surprisingly calm on the surface, but my mind races. I begin assessing, shuffling, scanning—not just the last three months, but my future as well. *Will I be OK financially? Do I have to list this job on my resume? Can I pretend it never happened?* I lean forward, "*Why* am I being fired?"

"It's not your performance. You've really thrown yourself into the work, have great organizational skills, a strong commitment." She pauses. "It's more interpersonal, really. I don't think you're a good fit with the team. And, you know, I'm leaving in a few weeks for the Portugal summit. Given your hesitancy to assist the male interns, I don't feel comfortable leaving you in charge."

I'm incredulous.

"You mean the gift shopping, and cooking?"

She remains silent. All I can hear is my own breathing.

I'M NOT SURE what happens at this point. Possibly I sit serene and appear to consider the situation with pause and great wisdom. Perhaps I'm in a state of shock and look like a freight train is headed toward me. Perhaps I faint, fall from my chair, and am splashed with cold water. All I know is that at some point I recover myself, and I've got something to say. "Can I give you some feedback?

Clara leans back in her chair, crosses her arms. "Fine. Let me have it."

"Not attack you. Just explain something. It's important to me, and important for the organization, too."

"Go ahead." She sighs.

"When you hired me, you said you were excited to have a Berkeley graduate on board, 'cause you knew I'd be capable. Then, my first morning on the job, you mentioned Berkeley again, and said it was a worry, because I might be obsessed with politically correct behavior."

Clara's arms clamp tighter across her chest, her chin is defiant. "I stand by that—the concept of P.C. behavior is ridiculous—it eliminates all dialogue."

"Yes. Thank you for restating it. *That's* what I want to explain. I've been confused for a while now that it could be good or bad that I'm from Berkeley... and I've been considering your perspective about people needing dialogue. At the lunch table you say things like 'Mexicans are corrupt, impossible to do business with,' and that 'Russians deserve an unstable government—such a thankless people.' And then, I notice, no one responds. It's not really dialogue. A week ago, I told you so directly. So, I guess, I'm wondering—is that why I'm being fired?"

Clara sits, watches me for a few minutes. Finally, she leans forward, unfolds her arms onto the table. "You said this was important to you *and the organization.* How exactly?"

"Well, it's illegal to make those statements in a place of employment. You must think that's as silly as being politically correct, but employees are supposed to report harassment to a superior. If the superior is the offender and there's no safe place for reporting, a lawsuit can be filed."

Clara stares, angry.

"You're my only option for reporting. If you fire me when I do that, I have grounds for a legal suit."

Silence.

"It's not a threat. But I leave, someone new comes, you start over again. You put yourself and the whole organization at risk."

We sit quietly again for a few minutes.

"It's interesting to hear you talk about this, Margaret. What do you call it? *Harassment?* Why not call it racism? It's what you mean. Do you know what it feels like to be a victim of racism?" She pauses, lifts an eyebrow. "I grew up attending International Schools throughout Asia. I was subjected to the worst forms of racism throughout my youth—violent sometimes. Dished out by other children who'd learned from their parents—*white* children. Who's victimized you in this lifetime, that you're so sensitive?"

And again, I'm not sure what happens here. It's either the fainting and cold splash of water, or a stunned silence, where I wait for the right answer. The answer that would talk about common decency, or some *special* kind of decency that trumps life experience. Maybe I'm still sitting there, waiting for the right answer.

THE PHONE RINGS in the kitchen. It's afternoon, but I'm in pajamas, holding a large mug of coffee. *Ring, Ring.*

"Hello?"

"Margaret, this is Fernando. I am so sorry. It is very important for me, I want to say, I enjoyed working with you very much."

"Did you... uh, *could you* say so to Clara?"

"I want to talk to you. Will you still come to Enrique's wedding? It would be so nice for you to come."

For all my confidence on the job, I am now plagued with doubt. My mind's been spinning questions for days. *Was I too stubborn? Too outspoken? Was it cultural difference that did me in? Gender?*

"... and my mother *does* come. In three weeks. We just make the ticket now."

Is it really bad to be a Dragon Woman?

"... and so I would like it, if you would come. To the wedding. And to my house for dinner."

I start to cry. I have to get off the phone before he hears me—will call him another day.

I've been fired.

I've never been so humiliated in my life.

NICU

Fontaine Roberson

IN THE DARK I can't tell what's dripping on my feet. My first sleepy thought is blood. Then I flip on the bathroom light and see that the front of my nightgown is soaked with breast milk and big drops of the precious stuff are hitting my toes. My instinct is to rush to Harper and hold her to my breast so she can eat. But my newborn daughter, born three months early, is in the neonatal intensive care unit at the hospital.

My breasts, prepared to feed a hungry full-term baby, are engorged with milk that I can't pump out fast enough even with the high-powered pump we've rented. The breast pump whirs and clunks as I watch my nipples being stretched down the shafts of the suction funnels and streams of milk shoot through the tubing into the bottles below. When I'm finished pumping, I gingerly pull myself out of the rocking chair, my C-section incision aching and pulling as I move. I walk downstairs to put the milk in the refrigerator, gripping the railing tightly and putting both feet together on a step before I lower myself to the next step. Back upstairs, I sit on the edge of the bed and carefully pull my legs up onto the bed. I look at Paul next to me. His face is scrunched like he's trying hard to sleep. My body feels so heavy against the mattress, so tired.

At 5:30 A.M. the alarm goes off. We pull on clothes, take the breast milk out of the refrigerator, and drive to the hospital without saying anything to each other. We're still stunned. A week ago today, at almost this hour of the morning, we drove this same route to the hospital with me moaning in pain—my liver swelling and blood pressure dangerously high from severe preeclampsia. Less than an hour later Harper was born.

THE DOCTORS AND NURSES call the neonatal intensive care unit the NICU. The doors are always locked and inside it's bright, noisy, and full of people at all hours.

Paul and I stand at the doors, push the intercom button, and look up at the security camera mounted on the wall. "It's Harper's Mom and Dad," I say to the camera. I still feel awkward calling myself "Mom" and I feel even more awkward when the nurses who are showing me how to change a diaper call me "Mom."

Inside the NICU our eyes adjust to the florescent lights as we stand at the long trough sink and scrub our hands with soap and antiseptic brushes. The skin on my hands is so dry it feels powdery. I scrub my hands like this every time I touch Harper and before I pump my breast milk every three hours.

Harper is asleep on her warming table and her nurse, Jennifer, stands beside her looking at her medical chart. Jennifer is my favorite nurse. She calls me Fontaine instead of Mom.

"Last night was a good night for her," Jennifer says. "She was pretty stable."

I sit down in the rocking chair and Jennifer puts Harper in my arms.

Her eyes are closed. We've only seen them open a few times. She's swaddled tightly in what the nurses call the "baby burrito." I put my face close to hers and whisper, "Mommy and Daddy are here, Harper. We love you." Paul kisses her on the top of her head. Jennifer takes out a gavage tube the size of a cocktail straw, pulls Harper's chin to open her mouth and runs the tube down her throat. Harper gags and turns red. The monitor over her bed beeps frantically and Jennifer reaches up to silence it.

She takes the breast milk I pumped earlier and pours it into a syringe attached to the gavage tube, and then holds it up so the milk drips down the tube and into Harper's tiny stomach. I look at Harper's face. We're not supposed to talk or sing while she's being fed because two sources of stimulation at once can overwhelm her.

THE DAY AFTER she was born, Paul and a nurse helped me into a wheelchair and brought me into the NICU to see Harper for the first time. She laid on a table the size of a briefcase under bright orange lights to warm her and treat her jaundice. Her eyes were covered with thick bandages to protect them from the lights. Her chest and belly were covered with electrode patches attached to lead wires that snaked around her and plugged into monitors filled with glowing lines, graphs, and numbers. She was naked except for a bandage-sized diaper.

She weighed just over two pounds, had almost no body fat. At twenty-eight-weeks gestation, the very beginning of the third trimester, the subcutaneous fat has just begun to develop. Her skin hung in wrinkles from her elbows and knees. My fingers touched her red, lanugo-covered back. "I'm sorry," I said softly.

"She likes it if you lay your hand firmly on her without rubbing," her nurse said. "She can't really process the sensation of rubbing." I cupped my hand over her chest. *My God, what's going on in her tiny mind? Is she scared of all these lights and noises and sensations? Is she in pain?* I put my pinky in her palm and she closed her fragile fingers around it.

THREE DAYS AFTER Harper was born I held her for the first time. I sat in a rocking chair with my hospital gown opened in the front while the nurse lifted Harper from the table, wires trailing behind her and laid her on my chest. I cupped one hand under her bottom and lay the other one on her back. Curled in a fetal position, her bottom rested between my breasts and her head tucked easily under my chin. Paul held the oxygen tube close to her face so she could breathe easily and her tiny pink hand fluttered against my breast. It felt like a rose petal.

When the nurse put her back on the warming table, Harper's earlobe was folded over and stuck flat to her head. There was no cartilage in it yet, just the flap of skin. I tenderly pulled it back into place and smoothed the red crease in the skin.

AFTER HARPER'S FEEDING Jennifer puts her back on the warming table. "It's time to change her feeding tube," she says. "You can get a good look at her while I do that." The feeding tube is taped to the side of Harper's face and a nasal cannula tube under her nose encircles her head too, so it's hard to see her face clearly.

Jennifer gently pulls off the tape. "It doesn't hurt like regular tape," she says. Harper doesn't seem to notice. Jennifer pulls the feeding tube out of her mouth, takes away the nasal cannula, and there it is. Harper's face. Her features are finely outlined against the bones underneath. She looks like a tiny old lady, the one she will someday become. I feel like I'm getting a glimpse of a Harper that I will never actually know.

Paul and I sit in the rocking chairs next to Harper's warming table and watch her sleep. After her feeding it will be a couple of hours before we can hold her again. Her plum-sized brain and immature nervous system can be stressed by almost anything, even just holding her for too long. When she's stressed, her heart rate goes down and her blood oxygen saturation falls, which causes wild beeping from the monitors that hang above the warming table. The nurses call this "having a spell."

While we're watching Harper, one of the resident doctors comes by and stands over our rocking chairs. "Hi Mom and Dad," he says, "I wanted to let you know that we did a head ultrasound last night. Common procedure for these babies to check for bleeding in the brain ventricles. We didn't see any bleeding, but we did see two small cysts, which could indicate injury."

I'm just staring at his mouth. "There's nothing to do for now," he says. "We'll do another ultrasound before she goes home to see if the cysts have changed or grown." He pauses and I'm still just looking at him. "If they get bigger there is some risk of developmental delays or cerebral palsy."

"OK, thank you," I say. I look at Harper asleep on her table. God, she's beautiful.

Complaining of Numbness

Jessica Byers

IT WAS JANUARY 11TH of my freshman year of high school. My mother
had been complaining of numbness in her left side for weeks, but she was
too busy to get it checked out. It was the holidays, we had the trip to New
York, and it was the final year of her MSW program. No time for doctor
visits. But something wasn't right. One morning she woke up and the
numbness was affecting her legs so much she felt wobbly. A friend had to
lend her a wheelchair to go to the emergency room.

She told me not to worry, to go to school and have a nice day. I went,
but about halfway through sixth-period chemistry, I was overcome with a
feeling that things were really not OK. I talked to my chemistry teacher,
who I'll always remember because his name was Mr. Gay and because he
was so kind to me that day. He told me to go right to the office, talk to Ms.
Pierce, and try to find my mother.

I did manage to track her down, and it turned out that she'd had X-
rays, which hadn't shown anything. She was being sent to another hospital

downtown for a CAT scan. I was fourteen and I didn't know what CAT scans were, so I didn't think much of it, except that this was a bit more of an ordeal than I'd expected. Hospitals were foreign to me. It had always been just me and my mother—and neither of us had ever been to the hospital as far as I could remember.

I found my way to Beth Israel Hospital, found my mother and her friend, Joanne, but the rest of that afternoon is a blur. Even in the face of being told that the CAT scan had found something near my mother's brain, and that she'd have to be admitted to the hospital right away for surgery to have it removed, I remained oblivious.

I called my best friend, Emily, from a bank of pay phones in a dimly lit brown-carpeted hallway. She seemed concerned.

"Do you think it could be cancerous?" she asked cautiously.

"What?"

"The growth, could it be cancer?"

"Oh no," I said. "I don't think so, they would have mentioned that, it sounded like nothing too serious."

Emily didn't sound convinced. Even though she was seven months younger, she had always been the smarter one, the one who knew more big words, the intellectual. Her father was a Shakespeare professor at MIT, after all, and she had two older brothers, one at Yale. Even when she was eight years old she used words like *facetious*, and had conversations with my mother that I didn't understand. But I always tried to be cool and pretend that I did. I didn't ask questions.

ON THE DAY my mother was admitted to the hospital, which would turn out to be the beginning of a six-week stay, I did not ask questions. Certainly I never asked if she could have cancer or if she could die before my fifteenth birthday. I preferred to believe that this would not disrupt my life, that there was nothing to be afraid of, that it would all be over in a week or two. And Emily chose to let it go that day, but better than I, she knew what we were in for.

The day before my mom had surgery, I found a copy of her Last Will and Testament lying around, certainly not intended for me to see. It said that she was leaving everything to me when I turned twenty-one, and there was a short list of people I could live with. The list included my grandmother and her husband, my uncle Peter, a cousin of my mom's, and two of her friends. At this point the possibility of her tumor being that serious, of her dying, had still not even occurred to me. I wrote it off as a standard safety precaution when someone has major surgery. I was already honing my ability to remain in denial.

ALL OF US sat in the big waiting room, quiet, a bit restless. My mother was in surgery. She'd been admitted to the hospital six days earlier. I knew that this was a big deal because my grandmother and her husband had returned early from their winter vacation in Costa Rica and my mother's older brother, Peter, had flown in from Seattle. He was a doctor, so although he was not very close to my mother, we needed him around to explain things.

One of Peter's daughters was my age and we'd spent some time together a few summers, making up dance routines to Debbie Gibson songs, exploring, and picking blackberries. But she was the only one in that part of the family I felt I really knew. Peter felt a bit distant. My grandmother told me years later that she thought the reason he never really warmed up to me was that he never understood my mother, and I was too much like her. She was the crazy one, the one who went to a tiny hippie college in Vermont and later convinced her parents to try dropping acid. She became the feminist single mother on welfare. He, on the other hand, went to the right schools, competed on the national swim team, got a fellowship to study in London, and became a successful doctor, speaking often at international conferences. He married another doctor and got a second home in the San Juan Islands. I remember Peter's kids always being busy with band practice, swim team practice, French cooking lessons, Italian classes. All that mystified me. I never played a sport, or an instrument for more than one semester, never spoke another language. Me, I was busy writing letters to politicians and taking the bus to DC for protests.

So we sat together, a disparate bunch: my grandmother and her lawyer husband, my grandfather and his wife Lucy, Peter, my mother's four best friends, me, and Emily, who would not leave my side until all this was over.

Dr. Blume finally emerged. He didn't smile as he gave us the run-down. He said that the growth was indeed malignant and my mother would need to undergo some radiation therapy. He threw out a bunch of other medical terminology that I didn't understand. I knew the news was bad because two of my mom's friends and my grandmother were crying, but I still didn't really get it. I didn't know the words "benign" or "malignant," and I didn't know what radiation therapy was, or why you would have it. Still, I didn't ask questions. I may have been naive, maybe had a limited vocabulary, but I was used to being told I was so mature for my age, so independent. I was used to getting the best grades in the class. I worked hard at maintaining that image.

Wednesday, January 17th, 1990
We went to see my mom in the recovery room. She had a large bandage on her head and most of her head was shaved except the far left side. She had an IV in her and a machine beeping above her and an oxygen mask on her face. She looked kind of Martian-like, but not too bad. We talked a little bit, though she was pretty groggy. They

wouldn't let her drink, so she was very thirsty. She was given these green spongy things to suck on and a little bit of ice.

This whole thing is so weird and stressful.

Thursday, January 18th, 1990

Around 3:45P.M. Emily came to the hospital and we sat in the admitting area by the windows and talked. Later we went up to my mom's room. She was looking a little better today, no tube and was slightly more with it. I told her I would braid the hair she had left.

We went home and Grami made hamburgers and salad for dinner. The three of us ate together. Then Emily and I chilled in my room. If I didn't have her, I don't know how I'd get through this. I can talk to her or just lie on her. She's so comforting.

SEVERAL NIGHTS LATER my Uncle Peter knocked on my bedroom door. He was the first to challenge my composure. He sat down on the floor, next to the huge poster of The Cure, as if he was just sharing some casual information. He talked to me about things like cells and radiation and chemotherapy for a few minutes. Then he said, "You know your mother is going to die, right?"

I did not know that. "Yeah, I guess so."

"We don't know how long she'll have, but we'll do everything we can to help her for as long as we can. It could be six months, could be a few years if we're lucky."

I nodded. I don't think I looked at him.

"I know, it's a shitty deal." And that's mainly what I remember him saying often after that.

That was the first time I cried about it, but even then I did so with a veil of denial over me. It seemed right to cry, but I was nowhere near comprehending the magnitude of the situation—nowhere near realizing that my mother was not just my mother; she was my whole family, she was my home.

Within a few weeks the topic of who I would live with after my mom died was being openly discussed. The main options were my grandmother and her husband, Charles, who were planning to retire soon anyway and might move up to Cambridge from Manhattan, or I could move to Seattle and live with Peter and his six overachieving kids—not an option in my mind. My own father was even less of an option. In fact, efforts were made to track him down and make him sign papers promising that he wouldn't try to get custody of me. He called later, wanting to speak to my mother, and she refused, said she was having a hard enough time without having to waste energy on that.

My father had left when I was two and half to go to India and be with his guru. He came back to visit once when I was six. The main memory I have of that visit is playing board games in my room and me cheating. He told me later he was proud of me because I did it so well. But after that he didn't come back and when people asked I said I didn't have a father. This wasn't out of hostility, it was a simple truth for me. The concept of fathers was foreign. I found it vaguely intriguing, but didn't lose any sleep over it. Still, when I was about eleven or twelve I got curious about who he was. My mother said he was an asshole and I shouldn't bother with him, but I wanted to see for myself, and she respected that. She treated me, by and large, like an equal—maybe more than she needed to. But she managed to track him down for me. He was taking care of a friend's farm in Chile. I wrote him a letter, asked lots of questions like what he did for a living and whether he'd remarried. He responded by saying his life now was about his love for this Indian man named Rajneesh. Not knowing who this was, and not getting much explanation from him, I interpreted this to mean he was gay, which was a more familiar part of my reality than Indian gurus.

So we wrote letters and sent pictures and when I was thirteen he came to visit for a weekend. My mom humored me and was nice to him. I have several memories of this visit. One was going out for Chinese food with both my parents. This is the only actual memory I have of the three of us ever being together. We sat in a big high-ceilinged restaurant with steaming platters of food and made polite conversation about what was going on in our lives. I wanted my dad to meet my friends, so he met Emily and then he met Anna. Anna asked him, in a casual conversational way, what he thought of Emily. He had no inkling of his role as a newcomer to my life, or of how to be appropriate with twelve- and thirteen-year-olds. He was all about openness, or his interpretation of that. He said Emily seemed pretty superficial because she was so obsessed with watching the Celtics on TV. He didn't know Emily at all, but he managed to hurt me by insulting my best friend. Out of what seemed like loyalty at the time, I told her that he'd said this, and she, of course, never forgave him. She was always protective of me, and wary of the man who had done less for me as a parent than she had done since we became friends when we were both six.

Emily was indeed a rare bird, but not a superficial one by any stretch. I remember very clearly the day we met. It was September, 1981. In those days, at our "alternative" public school, they mixed the Kindergartners and the first graders. That may have been the last year of that combination, but it was fortuitous for us. The day before school started, they had one of those meet-the-teacher days where our moms brought us in to see the classroom and meet everyone, so the first day of school would be less scary. Emily was five. I was almost six. I saw her there and immediately noticed her eyes. She had these sharp eyes that looked almost Asian in a way, but they were a greenish color. I looked at her and I was drawn in, intrigued by something in those eyes in whatever way a five-year-old can be—not on a conscious level, but still knowing I wanted to get to know her better—knowing we would be friends.

By fourth grade Emily and I were so close we'd written our own language and we spoke it in class to show everyone we had our own world. We wrote stories and made maps. We were the smart ones, and we knew it. We took the notes our friends passed and marked them up with red pen. Emily had asthma, and in junior high she got a serious trachea infection that was mistaken for an asthma attack until she almost stopped breathing. She ended up in the ICU for a week, barely conscious and on oxygen. I visited her every day. She gave me her stuffed polar bear and I carried it around with me, which was not a popular move among our peers. The nurses said I got her to talk when nobody else could. She got better, and she cried when I went on to high school and she didn't. We wrote each other long angst-ridden letters. But we would end up seeing quite a bit of each other the next year, even though it was the year we were at different schools.

TWO DAYS AFTER her first brain surgery, my mom turned forty-four. We had a party for her at the hospital, in a room down the hall from hers that they called the solarium. I made a big "Happy Birthday" banner on our new computer and hung it on the wall. My mom's best friend sent a clown to deliver balloons, but she was hardly awake when he arrived. She managed to perk later up for the party. There were probably twenty or thirty people, friends and family all bearing gifts. We had her favorite cake from Rosie's Bakery—chocolate with mocha frosting and layers of raspberry. Food would become extremely important to her in the months ahead, as it was one of the few things she could still control.

The last picture I have of my mom and me together is from that birthday party at the hospital. She's wearing a thick Irish wool sweater that a friend gave her. I'm leaning over her wheelchair with my arm around her and we're both grinning, despite the huge bandage on the shaved side of her head.

Nobody in the room mentioned that this could be her last birthday, but everyone was thinking it.

Following that first surgery, my mother stayed in the hospital for six weeks while various friends and relatives stayed with me at our apartment. The tumor had caused paralysis in the left side of her body, so at first I was most concerned about the immediate results of that: She would always be in a wheelchair, she would not be able to drive, she would need help with all kinds of things. I felt quite prepared to learn how to help her, to take care of things so that the two of us could be as self-sufficient as we'd always been. She spent the second half of those six weeks in rehab, learning how to function with her newly limited mobility. They kept saying she'd be home soon, and it kept taking just a little longer.

Finally, at the end of February, she did come home, but to an entirely different life than she'd left on January 11th. We'd outfitted the bathroom, as well as her bedroom, with all kinds of bars. We'd rearranged the furniture to accommodate her wheelchair. I was happy to have her home, and though there were lots of people around to help during the day, the evenings alone with her got hard.

Monday, February 26th, 1990

My mom definitely needs taking care of now. She's on five different medications to be taken four times a day. She's in a wheelchair and has a cane for the little walking she can do. She has use of only one arm, so there's this rubbery thing that goes under her plate when she eats so it doesn't slide around, and a plate guard so she doesn't push the food off the plate. She needs a lot of help around the house. There are four bars on the bathroom walls and a shower chair. I have to do most of the chores, which we used to split. Aside from regular cleaning and taking care of the cats, I have to make all the meals. My mother's friends are trying to help out a lot, but they can't move in. I wonder how she will do with the radiation.

MY MOTHER'S ILLNESS removed me from my previous reality of almost constant preoccupation with my social life, with picking apart and recording every social interaction. Detailing crushes—my own, Emily's, and everyone else's. Writing accounts of fights between friends, lies to parents, late night phone calls, parties. After my mother got sick and my life became consumed by that, I always had a feeling of being on the outside in social situations. I hovered, not really engaged. I wanted more than anything to be part of that high school world of parties and intense social drama. I did manage to get out to parties sometimes, to see people, so I don't know if people noticed that I was somewhere else, always wondering if my mom was OK, how long she'd be OK, and what was about to happen to my life.

The Instant I Changed My Answer

Mary Jane Kelly

REFUGE WAS THE WOODS. A soft dirt path through the hickory and oak. Quiet foreign beings paid attention here, and knew wise things. No one stared. Walking through the woods was moving through time and standing still in time. The sun shone differently and the trees felt you go by. Sometimes the creek was what to do, picking up rocks and looking for crawdads. Those days the sense of ease stretched far downstream, and soaked up the long life of the woods. The smells were the best, of rotted leaves. And the sparkle of sunlight on the water, distractions. The right kind of real. The water and the light, beautiful without struggle, and I could see that.

I had stopped dreaming. It was too real, the way we had to lie to ourselves. I turned inward with what I felt and what I saw. I began spinning the web that would contain my grief, and direct my angst to its least harmful place. With the strangest of twists, the web developed its own momentum, a self-generating cycle of hiding my grief, and hiding my grief at my hiding. And so refuge became the woods, where this protagonist wouldn't have to show up. Forget about me, please. The world could be the point. Mother believed in fairy elves and I believed in her, a quiet ethereal comfort, balm for the soul.

Our lives are overlain with the lives of others. Colored lenses give us pictures of one another like children playing dress-up. You must be the guy who drives the Matchbox BMW; I want the Volkswagen van. How simple a tragedy when one life turns down a road where no one can follow. "But we were playing," the rest will protest. And the lenses get out of balance. Light doesn't play on the water without a struggle anymore. Fairy elves become visions of clarity, beacons of truth, missionaries of civility and manners. Sometimes I wondered which was a distraction, which was real? Which beautiful, which something to hide? If there was a right answer, I was sure I had it wrong. Once I went back and could feel the ache in the forest I left there years ago.

See, mother was crazy. And she knew it the instant I had changed my answer, stopped believing in her. I sat down on the couch in her living room, and she looked at me point blank and said, "You think I'm crazy." I was stunned speechless. She knew the answers more solidly than I ever would. I was cast back into the forest, now with unknown dangers. She had been what I knew best. Now the reality of what I had known felt uncertain, and my assessment of her sanity or presence of mind was without evidence. I couldn't prove my case to her, and she saw more clearly what I was thinking than I would ever see in her thinking. I felt quite like a bug, pinned to a specimen board, identified with an undeniable label by my crazy mother.

Sometimes you notice a different reason for what you've gone through. You look back on turns in the road that you thought were fate, and they turn out to be unreal. It can happen years later, when you're vaguely reminiscing on passing some bend in the trail. The feel of the moment fills your senses, maybe the light shows off the season, or the dirt is dusty between your toes. And you realize that you didn't know it then, but you'd been changed. And you're changed again, now. Like tuning the radio, your heart is set to a new frequency. The world is different. It is right and good and clear as a bell, as if you'd passed through some truth beam that cleared away the illusion.

Reflections like these can hang suspended in time. It happens sometimes when someone has passed away. In a curious way, you can move around in the reflection as if it were an abandoned stage set. And you wonder if you could change the scene. And then you realize you have no way of knowing how the scene should have gone. And that real choices are limited, and their effect unpredictable. And that reality is something to navigate with a grain of salt, and that grief should not be taken so seriously, and that people can see you even when you're hiding.

Slaying the Dragon

Linda Hefferman

I'D FELT IT COMING ON, but didn't have the energy to fight it. A bug this strong, that could break through my multi-layered defenses—raw garlic swallowed whole; homeopathic pills made from my placenta; mega-doses of vitamin C—would require Napoleon's army to defeat it. And right now I couldn't muster the troops.

Maybe it was the weather that brought it on. It was April in Paris and even though the trees were dressed in baby green and frothy blossoms, the weather still waffled between seductively warm and blow-your-hat-off freezing. You could never tell which way it would go until you were outside, which meant we were constantly either scrambling to find our gloves or shedding layers like a snake.

Maybe it was the worry. At the end of June, my husband and I and our two kids would leave Paris, where we'd been living for a year, and move back to the States. But we had no place to live, no car, and, it was starting to look like, no work. My mind had been running laps around the 'what if' track at high speed. What if we couldn't find a place to live when we moved back to California? We'd heard from our friends that Silicon Valley had gone crazy—rents doubling, occupancy rates at 100 percent. What if Bill's consulting company didn't get any more contracts? What would we do for income?

Or maybe it was just plain exhaustion. Jon Luc, our seven month old, had decided that sleep was for wimps and was having no part of it. So neither was I. And we'd just said good-bye to one group of friends, who'd stayed for almost three weeks, and another family of four would arrive the next day. A few days after they left, Bill's mom would be coming to stay for ten days. Our house had served as a bed and breakfast for an endless stream of visitors since February.

"I feel like crap," I announced, slinging the baby backpack off my back and standing it up in the middle of the living room. Jon Luc had fallen asleep and his head lay on the padded shoulder strap at an awkward angle, his mouth agape like a cartoon caricature of a baby bird. His navy blue billed hat with the fuzzy earflaps had slipped over his eyes and his fleece suit bunched in thick folds around his shoulders. I kicked off my shoes, dropped my coat, and collapsed onto the couch. It was late, almost midnight. We'd just gotten home from a Friday night meander through the Marais, Paris' Jewish quarter, where bearded men in black suits wore their sideburns long and curly and deliciously pungent aromas wafted out of tiny kosher delis. We'd eaten at our favorite Middle Eastern restaurant. The food always came quickly—steaming falafel and garlicky yogurt, hot pita stuffed with grilled lamb and cucumbers—but the waiters vanished when we tried to get the check. By the time we'd finally paid, the baby had ripped the paper table cloth to shreds and Bill had told every Galant-the-Superhero-versus-the-Evil-Dragon-of-Fear-and-Illusion story in his repertoire to keep four-year-old Galen entertained. On the Métro ride home my flu symptoms started suddenly, the beginnings of a sore throat and an achiness that came on mysteriously, like my body had snuck off and competed in an extreme sporting event without my permission.

Bill looked up at me from across the room where he'd just peeled off Galen's clothes and was trying to cajole him into pajamas. "Really? You were fine earlier." Galen, who'd complained all the way home about his legs being tired, was racing naked around the living room, his arms outstretched like airplane wings, shouting that Nudeyman had broken out of the dungeon and was helping Galant the Superhero fight the dragon.

"I need to go to bed, like, *now*," I whined. "I'm so tired I can't even move." I didn't want to describe my other symptoms for fear that acknowledging them would give them a right to stay.

"You do look a little flushed," Bill said. He'd finally captured Nudeyman and was doing an expert job of both tickling and dressing his flailing body.

"Can you deal with Jon Luc?" I rolled onto the floor and leaned against the couch, resting my head on one of the green denim pillows. All of the sudden my teeth started chattering and I felt I'd never be warm again. And my bedroom seemed both right down the hall and a million miles away; like in a dream when no matter how hard you try, you can't get where you know you need to go.

Bill glanced at Jon Luc. "Sure. I'll just let him sleep in the backpack until I get this one in bed." He pulled a giggling Galen onto his lap. "Come on, Nudeyman. You're weak and powerless and you need to recharge your super powers. The only thing that will do *that* is sleep."

Thank God it's the weekend, I thought. Bill can deal with the kids for a few days.

THROUGH THAT NIGHT and into the next day, I drifted in and out of consciousness. I vaguely remembered nursing Jon Luc in the night, the clamping and pulling on my breast almost excruciating to my aching body. But I didn't know how well he slept or if Bill spent the night walking laps around the living room in the dark as I often did. At one point there was daylight in the room and Galen and Bill's voices drifted in from the kitchen as if from another world, far, far away. Then, what must have been later, I felt the bed move and Bill and Galen were sitting next to me, their clothes exuding the smell of cool fresh air. Jon Luc sat on Bill's lap, smiley and all dazzling dimples. He reached out his arms and I heaved myself up against the pillows and pulled him to my chest. He was heavy, like a fifty-pound sack of sand in my arms. "I've picked up the van from Hertz," Bill said. "I'm going to drive it to the airport to pick up Mary Ann and Coby. I'll take Jon Luc with me if you nurse him." I opened my nightgown, shivering to expose bare skin.

"I'm so cold," I whispered. I leaned my head against the pillow and closed my eyes. I could feel Jon Luc in my arms sucking on my breast, but it was as if it was happening to someone else's body.

"You're pretty sick, aren't you." Bill laid his hand on my forehead. I felt Galen's fingers slip into my hand and I shivered when their cool hands touched my hot skin.

Tears leaked from underneath my closed eyelids, their warmth turning cold as they trickled onto my neck, wetting the collar of my nightgown. I nodded, barely moving my head. Even so small a gesture seemed to take all my strength.

"What's wrong?"

I burst into big gulping sobs. "What're we going to do? Your company doesn't have any work—*nothing*. And we're leaving soon and we have nothing to go back to. I'm so tired of not knowing what's going to happen next in my life! And now I'm sick… I feel so awful. I can't even take care of the kids. What if I get Mary Ann or Coby sick on their vacation? Or their kids?"

Jon Luc looked up at me from my breast, his hand reaching for my mouth. He liked to put his fingers in my mouth when he nursed, and often smiled or giggled with the nipple in his mouth. I turned my head away from him toward the wall; at least I could try and avoid getting him sick.

"Why are you thinking of all that now? You're getting yourself all worked up when you need to be resting." Bill's voice was soft, like he was soothing a child. "You know it'll all work out. It always does." I turned my head and looked at his face through blurry tears. He was smiling, and in his eyes I could read the calm confidence with which he met every challenge, like it was more fun to live life that way. "Don't worry about getting anyone sick," he said. "You're just exhausted. I took an extra day off to spend with Coby and Mary Ann and we can wave to you from the door. I won't let them near you until you're better. And I can deal with the kids— Except for the boob part." He stroked my forehead and gently smoothed away the tears. "Now give me that baby and go back to sleep. You need to get better so we can have some fun with those guys."

He lifted Jon Luc out of my arms and plopped him on the changing mat on top of the white dresser next to our bed. "Now, little man, we'll get you all dry then you get to ride in the bumpy van to the airport. Doesn't that sound like fun?" Galen laid his head in my lap and I stroked his hair for a moment then he slid off the bed and stood next to Bill, making faces at Jon Luc, who squealed.

"Thanks, honey. I'm sorry." I slid down and pulled the covers up to my neck.

"What's Mommy got to be sorry about? It just means I get to hang out with my guys!" Bill blew a raspberry on Jon Luc's bare belly and he chuckled, that husky baby laugh that I usually found so funny.

SOMETIME LATER I DREAM that a fire-breathing dragon is attacking me. Mist surrounds me, mist so thick that it obscures any landmark or shape that would tell me where I am or which way to go to escape. Yet even though I can't see anything else, the dragon is sharp and clear, a crisp outline against the mist, like it has been cut from paper and placed on a grey background. The dragon is monstrous, the color of dried blood. Its long tail twitches like a separate entity, as if it's trying to detach itself from the dragon's body and slither off in the opposite direction. Its open mouth reveals multiple rows of jagged teeth, like a shark's. And from its black nostrils, tendrils of smoke curl out. I stand, facing the approaching dragon, and in my left hand I hold a broad sword, sharp and lethal and shiny, a weapon clearly capable of killing, if only I could lift it. But I'm so tired, too tired, the weight of the sword dragging my body to the ground, pulling me down to my knees until I'm crouching. The dragon moves slowly closer until it looms over me, its eyes menacing. It's even bigger than I'd thought at first and seems to be growing. I place my other hand on the sword hilt and try to lift it with both hands. But the sword won't move. It takes too much strength. And I'm so tired.

I'll just lie down for a little while. I lay my head on my forearms, still clutching the sword with both hands, and close my eyes. "Just let me sleep," I whisper. *I'll die. The dragon will eat me. But I don't care; as long as I can sleep…*

I wake a little later and open my eyes. The bedroom is darker than it had been when Bill was there and I realize it must be dusk. But my eyelids won't stay open. Something is dragging me back.

My eyes close then open to the mist. I am standing now, the dragon still looming over me, exactly as it was before. I still grip the sword tightly, though only in my left hand, like at the beginning of the dream. But still my arm feels heavy and weak and I know I lack the strength to lift it. I wonder why the dragon did not kill me as I slept at its feet. Maybe it can't see me, or its sense of smell has been dulled from all that smoke.

The voice comes from nowhere and everywhere and from somewhere inside me all at the same time: "You can tell the dragon to go away." A simple statement; no fear, no urgency for my dire situation. It comes again: "Just tell it to go away." *But I'm so tired…* I try, again, to lift the sword. Not even the slightest budge. The dragon's tail sweeps back and forth as if in slow motion. I look up, directly into its mouth and teeth. They are getting closer as it leans down, its mouth open and right over my head.

"Go away," I say. My voice is weary, lacking conviction. The dragon's head stops moving. "Go away," I say again, this time a little more forcefully. The dragon raises its head on its long neck. Then it turns and slowly shuffles off into the mist. My grip on the sword hilt releases and I wait for the clatter it will make as it hits the ground. But there is no sound. In the distance I can just see the dragon disappearing into the mist before it dissolves into nothingness. I look down at my feet and there is no sword, just my empty hand in the mist. Then the mist turns to darkness and everything goes blank.

I WOKE TO A DARK ROOM and a clammy nightgown against my wet skin. My hair was damp on my face, but my body felt relaxed, no longer cold or achy. I could hear laughter from the living room muffled by the closed bedroom door, and the rise and fall of voices in conversation. Coby and Mary Ann had arrived. I thought about the dragon, whose image seemed too vivid for an ordinary dream. It was so menacing, yet all it had taken to send it away had been a simple command: "Go away." *Is it that simple?* I wondered. *Will all my fears go away that easily?* Maybe Bill was right. Everything will work out.

The door opened and a shaft of light from the hall fell across my face.

"How are you doing?" Bill asked.

I smiled. "Much better."

Time

Lori Maliszewski

WHEN THE PRESIDENT of my division at work dropped dead of a heart attack at age fifty-one on the thirteenth hole of his private golf course, it was incomprehensible. Sure, he was overweight. Sure, he smoked. But fifty-one? That was too young to die.

A work colleague and I looked at each other in shock. We were both forty-five.

"Can you believe it?" Dee asked from her cubicle.

"No, I can't. What would you do if you knew you only had six years to live?"

For once, Dee was at a loss for words. She just slowly shook her head from side to side. No easy answer.

I've always been time conscious. Those who know me well might even say I'm pugnacious about time. I care about being on time and not wasting it. I inherited this trait from my father, who thought being on time meant being ten minutes early. The fact that my husband was almost two hours late for our first date was not the most auspicious beginning, but his other charms made up for his tardiness. After sixteen years of marriage, we've both made compromises in this regard, but it's still my nature to be wrapped up in time.

I will purposely arrive fifteen minutes early for a doctor's appointment, only to wait thirty minutes past the appointed time to be called in. I hate walking into a movie when the previews have already started. I'll figure out how much time it will take to reach a given destination then add more time, just in case something happens along the way. I was the only one I know who was satisfied when, after 9/11, the airlines required you to check in two hours early for domestic flights. Finally, I could be as early as I truly wanted to be.

Saving time is just as important as being on time. I scrutinize all of my to-dos, whether personal or professional, then categorize and group them for most efficient implementation. I timed different routes for my commute from West Linn to Wilsonville—seventeen minutes vs. nineteen minutes… and we have a winner! When finding a space in a crowded parking lot, driving around looking for a spot close to the entrance is a waste. Just park in the first space you find and walk; you'll save time.

Time is more important than money. Not to be squandered. My husband lovingly calls me an efficiency expert and I bear that moniker proudly, like a badge of honor.

WHEN I ASKED DEE what she would do if she only had six years to live, I knew what she didn't, that I was sick. I'd been steadily losing weight, and had undergone test after test to find the cause. Less than a month later, I was diagnosed with a rare form of pancreatic cancer; not quite as deadly as the normal kind, but incurable and ultimately terminal.

I couldn't help but ask my oncologist, "How much time do I have?"

"We can't tell you for sure, but it could be three to five to seven years or more."

The commodity to which I had attached so much value was truly endangered.

The rhetorical question I had posed to Dee just a few weeks earlier was now real for me; what does one do when given a limited amount of time to live? I asked for and got a lot of opinions:

"I'd strap my butt to an airplane and travel the world!" My wanderlust friend Tina advised.

"Follow your passion!" Rita said. And I realized I'd never identified a true passion. Add that to my to-do list: discover passion.

"At least you don't have kids you have to worry about leaving behind," said Don, father of two sons. Even though that stung, bringing to the surface the long-buried pain of being unable to have kids, he was right. It was impossible for me to imagine the heartache of leaving children.

"Quit work!" others advised. Yeah, but work was all I'd ever done. *Was work my passion?*

"I'd seek moments of bliss," said Keith. Nice concept, but not exactly something I could sink my teeth into.

"Take the summer off and just play," advised my wise friend Sue. So I did half of what she suggested and left work on disability leave nine months after my diagnosis.

NOT WORKING WAS NO EASY TASK. I was used to being somewhere at a certain time, had come to expect a certain amount of recognition for my accomplishments, and I always knew exactly what to do with my time. Now, given my situation, it seemed even more important not to waste time. I created new to-do lists based on years of accumulated home action items that never quite got done: Clean closets, oil the kitchen cupboards, paint the laundry room, organize photos, get rid of all unwanted items, tidy up the yard. Maybe this organizing was just a way to avoid the cluttered chaos of my mind that asked the same question over and over again, *Do I work or not, and if not, then what?*

After all of my ruminating, I sought out my husband for his gentle honesty and advice.

"What do you think I should do?"

"I think you should quit working." He never wavered from this point of view.

Either by luck or fate, I had purchased disability insurance several years earlier, which provided me a portion of my income should I become disabled. Given the catastrophic nature of my illness, I was eligible for disability leave.

"Tell me why again."

"Honey, I think you're going to live for a very long time. But what happens if it's just three years? Do you want to spend that time working? I think you should quit and consider it an early retirement."

"But what happens if I live fifteen years and I quit now? Will I have made a mistake?"

"No, work is consuming all of your energy. It won't be a mistake," he promised me.

With that in mind, over the summer I started to build some new structure for my life. I went to yoga classes twice a week, I scheduled lunch with friends to make sure I didn't get too isolated, I started attending a writing workshop, and did art therapy with my friend Patricia.

Through all of this, I started to envision what my life might be like if I didn't return to work. I was already much less stressed out and had shifted much of my energy and focus to health enhancing activities. It was a huge breakthrough when I was finally able to say to myself and others, "I'm eighty-five percent sure I'm not going back to work." And that's where I got stuck for weeks. Even I knew that this was a ridiculous stopping point, so I decided to see a therapist to help me through the final 15 percent of my decision making.

Ruth came into the lobby to take me back to her office. She was of average height, had frizzy, dull-brown hair, wore no discernible make-up, and had a matronly body somewhat hidden by a long flowing dress. She had a comfortable, lived-in look and I just knew that if I felt the need to crawl into her lap for solace, that it would accommodate me.

"I have two objectives in seeing you," I explained. "I want to make a final decision about work; and if I decide not to return, then I want help with understanding how to build a new life."

It didn't take her long to see how identified I was with the concept of work. In a few sessions, she helped me understand that my work was just changing. Instead of high-tech marketing, it was my job now to create my own well-being. Somehow she convinced me that working on myself was valid and worthwhile.

Our fourth session together she said to me: "There's something about you that's really been bugging me."

"What's that?" I asked, figuring it couldn't be too bad. She must have taken some therapist oath not to screw people up more than they already were.

"You came to me and told me you were dying. But what I see in front of me is a woman who is engaged in life. Do you really feel like you're dying?"

I thought about it for a moment. The doctors told me I was dying. They said I had a limited amount of time to live. But do I feel like I'm dying?

"No." I finally answered. "I don't feel like I'm dying." Both of us understood what an important truth this was for me to acknowledge. If I wasn't dying, then I must be living.

Around this same time, I had a conversation with the friend of a friend that clinched the decision for me. Kay is a massage therapist and artist, and on a different path than all of my friends in high tech. I told her what a hard time I was having making a decision.

"I think that if you go back to work you'll die sooner than if you don't," she said.

The truth of her simple assertion left me breathless, work meant death. Looked at that way, the choice was easy.

Not returning to work was still a certain kind of death for me. It was the death of a way of life no longer appropriate for me. And out of that death came the opportunity for a new life. The life I'm building now.

I'D JUST COME into the back yard from a morning walk with Rudy, our chocolate lab. It was so unusual to have such a warm and dry day in February that I just had to sit down for a moment and feel the warmth of the sun directly on my face. I planted myself in a chair and felt the heat of the sun begin to penetrate my cold winter bones. I noticed that the buds of the camellia bush next to me were just barely containing their fuchsia blossoms and it wouldn't be long now before they emerged from their leafy womb. A little brown bird hopped about on the branches of the bush and I thought I'll have to ask Sara what kind of bird that is. Sara is my neighbor and has all sorts of feeders to attract birds. My eyes meandered around the yard and I noticed the yellow and purple crocuses that had been blooming for weeks and the daffodils that were just now raising their heads from their deep, prayerful bow. I closed my eyes and let the sun seep further into me. Roots grew out of my body and into the chair as I found myself completely tranquilized by the sun. I should at least get up and pull some weeds, said my former list-making, efficiency-expert self. No, came the answer as the roots grew even deeper. I gave in to the will of my body and just sat. As often happens when I'm still, thoughts of my illness and death crept uninvited into my mind like a cold fog. A wave of loss and sadness rolled through me. But the sun had something else to teach me that morning and gently nudged my sad thoughts away. In that moment of my communion with the sun, and the birds, and the blossoms, I realized that I had all the time in the world.

AND GO HOME AGAIN

15 Reno Winter Highway

Rachel Indigo Cerise Baum

RUNNING I-5. Red Bluff. Guy drives an old Bentley. Resembles Ron Jeremy. I try to like him. I don't care anymore.

"Are you hungry?" My hopes up. His voice sounds kind. He buys me a burger and fries. I'm nervous when I order the chocolate shake too. Don't want to push my luck. That truck driver is out on the highway somewhere. Two packs of smokes and five bucks.

I don't know about this kind of house. Gravel driveway. Fresh paint. Manicured lawn. Red shutters. Black wrought iron door with keyed lock before he opens into his ulterior. Black leather couches and matching armchairs complement his antiques. Huge green leaf plants fill his den, like the jungles John Wayne waded through in Green Beret.

"You must be tired." He hands me a goblet of warm brandy.

After my shower he buttons me up into a white dress shirt warm from his dryer. He opens the hide-a-bed. Tucks me in. "You must be sleepy."

I'm warm and exhausted. My legs and arms are ghosts that won't move. When I think about how to move the thought goes away. I don't want to sleep when I see his shirt unbutton, and I can't think how my arms and legs used to move.

"Do you mind?" he slips his hindquarters under the covers. His arm wraps around my neck.

"I'm tired."

He tightens his grip on my neck. He is not a truck driver. There's an X that marks the spot where I was lost and found myself. Night.

I'M ON A BRIDGE when the next man stops. I've leaned way over the rail and thought about it. I turn and look at him. He drives a sedan, wears a fresh pressed business suit and looks so damn straight I almost laugh out loud. He opens the passenger door. I get in.

"Where are you going?"

I tell him, "I'm going back home. I'm going to Oregon. Do you know how to get there?"

When we stop, he shows me which way to go, and how much closer I am. He opens his wallet. I freeze. I hold onto the door, but I'm ready to run. I don't know what he wants from me, but I haven't had any breakfast yet, and I'm starved. He sets a ten dollar bill on the passenger seat. He turns and looks forward. His hands stay on the steering wheel. When I reach for the money, he sits completely still. I wonder what this fuckin' rapist's game is. I lean over and snatch the money. I back away from his car and keep my eyes on him. He turns and smiles, says "Jesus loves you." He drives on.

In the next town, I buy baloney and bread and wolf it down. There's no way to keep mayonnaise, but I consider the deli's plastic knives.

I think about what sedan man said. It means nothing to me. I believe him.

Childhood Bedroom

Hope C. Hitchcock

SHE STARED AT HER NAKED IMAGE for quite some time. Maybe her mother was right. Maybe she did look pregnant, maybe she really had gained 100 pounds. She hadn't had a full length mirror in ages, but now that she was back home in her old room, she did. It was shocking. Shocking what a couple of years without a mirror will do to you. She shook herself and watched the waves of flesh ripple over the length of her tiny frame. The sight made her feel nervous and calm simultaneously.

The break-up had nearly ruined her. She couldn't easily tie her shoelaces anymore. She was addicted to cigarettes, sugar, salt, fat, weed, booze. And she was broke. A year ago, she'd quit her job. Her first real job with insurance, paid vacation, a 401K, the works. She'd quit abruptly, after a year of smiling and saying, "Oh sure, no problem, I'd love to" while taking it in the ass from her demon of a boss. She'd left the office exhilarated, free.

She went out and got herself a job at a movie theater. She worked three nights a week for minimum wage. She smoked pot with her manager in the projectionist's booth. After the shows started, she and the boys mixed rum with the free coke and made hot batches of popcorn with extra butter topping. She sat on the stoop of the theater and licked salty butter and dirty money residue off her fingers. Drowned the kernels in rich brown syrupy soda and chain-smoked *Born Frees*, the cheapest cigarettes she could find. She and her roommates threw big parties at the house and she paid for the kegs on her credit card. When everyone got her back with cash, she paid her rent. She put her groceries and drinks on the cards. When her phone got shut off, it was more of a relief because the creditors were calling everyday, sometimes they'd call at night. Her roommates laughed with her when she smiled and said, "Uh, no, she's not in right now. I don't know when she'll be back. She may have moved."

But really, she was a little scared to be hunted like that. She had nightmares. She wanted to die.

So when her mom came for a visit, took one look at her and said, "What's happened? Who did this to you?" with such anguish she couldn't quite say.

She wanted to blame it on the old lover, but loyalty prevented her, so she just burst into tears, big soft shoulders shaking.

HER MOTHER STROKED her thinning hair and said, "Maybe you need to come home for awhile, get yourself straightened out."

"OK," she sobbed.

She sold everything. She watched her beautiful clothes scatter across the city, maybe even across the bay. Strangers left with her Mexican pottery and one nice teacher bought most of the plants. She couldn't figure out a way to pack up the treasures. It felt overwhelming to say good-bye to her friends, the old lover, that city she still craved. Her mind was unresponsive.

She got a yeast infection. She cried a lot. Her mother came to drive the van across state lines. They made one last trip to Goodwill and she handed the men martini glasses, a children's book she'd meant to send to someone, her unicorn collection, ribbons, colored pencils, her old velvet couch. A suitcase with who knows what inside. Her mother stood by, tight-lipped. Angry that so many things she'd bought as Christmas gifts were headed to the Goodwill aisles.

"You gave away all your nice things and you're saving this *shit?*" her mother yelled as she watched her load a box of full old empty plastic CD cases.

Then her mother actually broke down in tears when she packed the sign into the van. She had to bring it, though. She and the old lover had found it on Polk Street. They'd walked in the rain, one of the last walks they took together. The fish and chips shop was being gutted, torn down. It was an authentic fish and chips place. They wrapped everything in newspaper and they used a very particular brand of cheap UK oil to fry everything. The smell of that place made the lovers grip hands and smile because they met in London, kissed that same grease off each other's lips. On this day the rain poured over their heads and the disemboweled shop. She wanted to cry because she knew it was ending. She no longer felt comfortable gripping hands. The smell was gone. The old lover looked at her, she wanted to kiss her again.

"Let's take the sign," she said smiling.

"But it won't fit on the bus."

"C'mon, I'll pay for a cab."

Like magic, a cab soared over the hill and right to the curb. They hefted the sign into the trunk and it sat in her room for the whole summer. Her mother only saw the grime and frayed cords. A few plastic letters had gone missing. It read, " ish & Ch s $2.00." She would not leave it. She stamped her foot on the sidewalk like a toddler. Her mother watched in horror, but she was adamant.

She carried her last plant on her lap and she cried up I-5 and all over 99. She cried when she landed in her childhood room and cried harder when she tried to sleep in her old narrow bed. She rolled over the first night and fell right off. Her dad went to work in a suit and tie and left her in her bathrobe, crying on the couch. She was still in her bathrobe when he came home for lunch. They let her cry for a few months.

She didn't want to see anybody. She didn't tell anyone she'd moved home and she rarely left the house. She changed her address to General Delivery and refused to give the credit card companies her new number. The letters had become threatening. They were mentioning lawyers. At night she felt them nipping at her heels, drawing blood. Her parents didn't know. She lived in fear that one day the creditors would track her here. Debt was a grave sin in this house, second only to murder or rape. She owed $16,000. Maybe more. It had been a long time since she last looked at the amount owed. What had she been thinking? She hadn't really. The last time she attempted to come up with a plan, she got as far as a bus ticket to Kansas. She wanted to lie down in an endless field, one long brown horizon, and let the earth swallow her back. She wanted to buy heroin and die in Kansas.

She rolled up some towels and placed them at the base of the door. She brought the shitty plastic bong out from the closet and put her last remaining nug in the bowl. She sat on the little bed naked. The dirty water bubbled, the smoke lifted and she pulled it into soft pink lungs. If they still were soft and pink. Her breasts lay like dead sea lions over her huge belly. She had new red stretch marks. Like a pregnant woman. Big violent tears. She smiled a biter smile. She never planned on having children. She always thought she'd be spared this indignity.

That night she lay in bed. Her dollhouse stood as sentry. The box of CD cases growled at her feet, little restless puppies. The old fish and chips sign huddled in the corner begging for change and the framed photos sighed with deep contentment. She stroked her belly while watching it rise high above her with each inhalation. She did not know what it was inside her, she only knew it must be born.

Adrift

Emily A. Phillips

AFTER I GRADUATED COLLEGE, I lived paycheck to paycheck working overtime as a caregiver in the homes of women with developmental and physical disabilities. I worked twenty-four-hour shifts that started at 7:00 P.M. and didn't end until 7:00 P.M. the next day. Twenty-four hours of routine times three. My days slurred together with hygiene schedules and hours and hours of game show episodes on the PAX channel. I did their laundry, vacuumed while they screamed at me to stop, dusted the photos and knick-knacks their absent families sent, scraped together dinners with ingredients the other caregivers bought. Dinners that barely followed their diets, dinners that they aspirated in their mouths, that I had to wipe up off their bibs and out of the wrinkles in their necks. I came home to my basement room feeling empty, vacant, desperate for someone to take care of me, for someone to take pity on me, to tell me I was better than this.

When my sublet was up, I moved into my old professor's basement. I stayed there a month before I decided with resignation and guilty relief to give up on trying to support myself and move back home. I thought it would provide me with the stability to figure out what I wanted to do with my life. It was a long shot, but I was hopeful. I didn't have much to lose. I hated my job and I had no one to come home to. Caroline and I had broken up a few months earlier. She'd moved to San Francisco, but we still talked, long tearful conversations wherein we deconstructed every facet, every angle of what had gone wrong and why. We couldn't let go, but we agreed that it was time to take a break, to give each other "space." When I thought about moving home, I envisioned sleeping in, free rent, walks in the woods miles from anyone, my mom cooking supper, hugs in the morning and kisses at night. My parents were ecstatic at the idea. I rationalized moving back with all sorts of hopeful long-term plans. I would attempt to foster a relationship with my dad, I would come out to my family once and for all, I would figure out what to do with the rest of my life. It was going to be great. It was something I *needed* to do. So I packed up all my possessions and drove across country.

For the next eight months I rarely slept through the night. I was used to a full-size bed. The one in my old room was a cot-size twin in a high sleigh frame, a hand-me-down from my grandmother who'd been moved to a nursing home to wait out her last years, to prepare for the inevitable, to be cooked for, cared for, and cleaned up after by young women like me, certified nursing assistants barely scraping by. My toes hung over the edge when I lay on my stomach. If I sprawled, my arms and legs hung off the sides. If I slept on my side, I felt like I was perched on an edge. It was like sleeping in a coffin raised three feet off the ground. I thought about my grandmother in that bed. Did she ever think about its coffin-likeness? How depressing, how lonely, to confine your dying body to this narrowness, this subsistence, just barely taking up your allotted physical space.

THE FIRST FEW WEEKS I woke every night from dream—I was clinging to the edge of a cliff. I was paralyzed, unable to stop myself from falling. My body was dead weight, as in a coma, a tightly cocooned body bag, my eyes drugged closed, resolutely unable to open. I felt myself slipping, like a heavy envelope sliding from between a stack of other envelopes, down a dark shoot, fluttering from a dark abyss to land soundlessly with a start, awake in my bed, gripping the sides of the mattress.

The dreams continued night after night and I began to anticipate them. I became so familiar with them that I began to meditate on the images that I woke with. I clung tightly to my narrow raft of mattress and skated that edge of lucidity between subconscious and conscious for as long as I could, trying to fixate on the images that the feelings evoked rather than the feelings themselves: A dark black sea; looking up from a deep pit; eternal starless, moonless, endless nighttime; shipwrecked doom; gasping for air on an unfamiliar shore.

I was depressed and I knew it.

I practiced keeping my mind vacant, like a bolt of black silk stretching out eternal. Eventually, it always fluttered and collapsed into a fit of wrinkles, the surrealism buckling into analysis of *what did it all mean?* The country stillness, bright with moonlight, was irritatingly quiet and the clock's ticking echoed around me, counting down the seconds until I imploded. Nights I lay awake, plotting my next move, attempting to harvest the last shreds of hope that moving back home might pay off somehow. Days, I attempted to be productive. I looked for work, I researched graduate schools, internships, literary journals. Fall set in and I took up knitting again, spent hours on the couch with my mom, our elbows flying, needles jerking, spinning out yards of cloth in silence, the TV shouting in the background. I gave in to how easy it was to do nothing. I stopped reading, stopped writing, stopped thinking about the future. I absorbed myself in knitting, naps, and the television, watching re-runs of *I Love Lucy* and MTV's *Rich Girls*. I talked with Caroline every night, attaching myself to her like an anchor, a lifeline to a life of freedom and non-judgment that I'd once had.

One night over a cheery bottle of red wine, when my dad seemed to be in a good mood, I told him. "Dad, I have something I need to tell you. Mom knows, but you don't." I said it as plainly and as bluntly as the truth is. "I like girls, dad."

His eyebrows knitted together and he seemed confused. He told me he didn't understand.

I repeated myself. "I like girls, dad."

He still didn't get it.

"Lesbian, dad." I knew he would never understand the concept of queer.

His mouth pursed and he looked stumped. After a long pause, he told me he thought it was a difficult path, that it was just a phase, that I should think about picking a different lifestyle.

I shook my head and told him that I'd been like this for a long time, that I was OK with it.

He paused again, patted my hand, and told me he just wanted me to be happy.

Expecting anger, shouting, and tears, I was surprised at how easy it had been. I shrugged and thought *Wow, my dad's cooler than I thought.*

A FEW WEEKS LATER Caroline came to visit for Thanksgiving. We slept on an inflatable mattress on the floor of my room because my bed was too small for the two of us. We had clumsy muffled sex and tensed up every time we heard my parents walk by my room. She had fresh scabs on the inside of her thighs and I wordlessly acknowledged them, brushing my fingers lightly over the scars she'd inflicted on herself. I knew she didn't like to talk about it, so I stayed quiet. But I couldn't help thinking about the first time she'd cut. The circumstances, the plot of the horrible break-up that led up to the harvesting of her own self-worth. Pain for pain, as if they cancelled each other out somehow. Call it vengeance, call it sadistic, call it sick or whatever you want. I secretly blamed myself for those cuts, as if I was the one holding the razor blade.

Over the week, we spent as much time as we could out of the house and the entire time my father didn't say a word to her, not even a thank you for the sausage she'd bought him, which he stuffed his face with while we watched, ignored. Not even a goodbye or a wave as we walked to the car to drive her to the airport. I was devastated, perplexed by his behavior, ashamed, and guilty that I felt I was unable to say anything to him about how he had treated Caroline.

Unable to confront him, I lapsed into a childish attitude reminiscent of my adolescence. He responded in kind and we set about ignoring each other. My hackles raised whenever he entered the room. I treated him as tersely as he'd treated Caroline. It was passive aggressive, but I was confused and hurt. I spoke with my mother about it, but she only turned the conversation to God's plan for me. She told me how my plans would continue to crumble unless I gave myself over to His will, whence I might bask in his glory and benevolence. In order to reap His rewards, she said, I would have to admit that my sexual preference was a product of my willfulness, my hubris, my folly.

One night over soup, unable to contain my anger anymore, I confronted my dad: "It really hurt me that you couldn't even say hello to her. She was here for nine days and you didn't say one word to her."

It was out of my mouth before I could think twice, and I couldn't believe it. I must've been exploding. A glass house on fire. Mom's homemade vegetable beef soup turned sour in my mouth in the heavy silence that followed. I felt sick to my stomach and full of angry tears. They welled into a lump in my throat and at the sign of conflict my heart rate jumped to 135 beats per minute. I swallowed hard and took a slow breath. My stomach's pit burned. I'd come this far, so I took a step further. "You could at least have been respectful and acted civil."

He threw up his hands and started, "Emily!"

I cringed. All of my life I'd heard this from my dad—*Emily!*—His aggravation was palpable and the control it gathered was abrupt, the silence fuming. My mom and I held our breath.

He dropped his head heavily, shaking it slowly from side to side. "I just can't condone such a thing."

"I'm not asking you to condone it. I'm asking you to be polite, to say hello, to be happy for me."

"I can't be happy for you, Emily. The path you're on is destructive. It will only lead to sadness."

I paused. "This is who I am, dad, and I'm happy with her." I paused again and walked out on the limb in front of me. "I'm sorry I can't be the person you want me to be."

"Me too, Emily," is all he said. "Me too."

It hit me like a ton of bricks. My face crumbled. The hand of cards I'd been playing, the poker face I'd kept up all those years folded. I'd gambled and lost big. I looked down, looked into the soup, greasy red, olive green peas floating like buoys. Choking back the stream of sour tears, I salivated. I took a bite of soup and as if eating his words, it curdled in my mouth. I felt nauseous. I felt defeated. I felt free…? Free like an exile. Like an empty balloon, sailing above the table, looking down on all those bent heads, placemats, and green lattice work at each bowl's edge. The bright red shiny soup blurred. Fat tears fell like rain drops.

Staring into that soup I went numb and my brain felt a letting go. Like a raft, I set sail and drifted out onto a lake.

I am like an island washed off the sea of its shore. I stand alone. I stand in opposition. I find myself in conflict on my own soil, with my own flesh and blood. Surrounded by calm dark seas it dawns on me that the charade is over, that finally we're all in the know, that this conflict won't ever be solved because he isn't willing to cross this water, to meet me part way. I know that I will have to accept how he feels and move on, but always feel between us that wall, that distance. And solution or not, that *is* the resolution.

Dear Caroline,

This letter will self-destruct as soon as I am finished writing it.

Imagine you begin to have a recurring dream. It's plotless, haunting. Psychedelic nightmares of dark, ominously looming thoughts, self-doubts, dread, and disappointment. They wake you suddenly, your mind heavy and groggy, slung weighted and filled, like a net of fish tossed up onto the shore of the mattress. I know you know how I feel. You cling tightly, gaping and bleary-eyed, to the mattress edge, gasping for water, cast out of the sea of sub consciousness onto the shore of consciousness. Your stirring soul, part in, part out, backstrokes the thin line of tension that separates the two, water and air, asleep and awake. You are a lone boat on an empty beach. Awake and leached with doubts about yourself, you feel despondent, like no matter what you do you are cursed to fail, to be miserable, melancholy, dissatisfied. These are my dreams. Are they yours, too?

I have begun to question if my parents aren't maybe right. They believe that I am making a desperate mistake loving you. Their disapproval cuts me more deeply than I thought possible. The knife's tip irritating the very marrow of who I know myself to be. I have begun to secretly question if I will ever be happy, if I will ever become the person I am meant to be, if I really am queer, and if God's way is really as easy and pain-free as my mom promises. Their disapproval makes everything harder. It makes it harder to have faith in my future, it makes it harder to feel wholly happy or satisfied. More than anything, it makes it incredibly hard to live here, to love them as they should be loved. I feel a subtle chewing pain in their presence, in the silence after your name, in the absence of examples to follow. I feel completely alone, shipwrecked. I have begun to drink in my room, where I hide the bottles behind the bed.

I have failed. I have failed you, myself, my parents, and God. This is how I feel. I know it sounds dramatic, but here in this world, failure is the prognosis and the only cure it seems is to shape up and conform, or to escape. So I'm tying my raft to you, my tugboat, S.S. Caroline. Let's move to Portland, so you can be close to your folks and I can be far from mine. Let's run away together and be exiles. Let's pretend my doubts about you and myself never happened and that all the heartache we've caused each other won't get in the way of starting fresh. Let's pretend that we aren't just holding onto each other because we're scared to be alone. Let's pretend that all we need is each other and that I'm still in love with you. Let's pretend that everything will be fine.

Resurrection

Jean Braden

IT WAS 9:30 P.M. as my husband, Gary, and I drove to my brother Bob's home in Aumsville, Oregon. I was shaking, taking deep breathes, and my eyes hurt from crying; it had been a long hard hour and a half drive. Gary and I were both caught up in our own thoughts and only talked occasionally. My father had drowned in Detroit Lake that afternoon, on the opening day of fishing season in 1983. He was seventy-three years old.

The house glowed with lights and many cars were already parked in the long driveway when we arrived. We pulled in behind the last car and walked slowly toward the house. Under the light by the barn I could see Mom and Dad's camper and boat. Bob had brought them home when he'd gone up to Detroit Lake to get Mother.

Both of my brothers, Bob and Fred, were waiting for me on the walkway. We wrapped our arms around each other and cried together. "I wish I'd told Dad that I loved him," Bob said.

Fred nodded.

I tightened my arms around them. "Dad knew you loved him," I said softly. "He knew it." I thought back to Mother's Day when Dad and Mom had come to our home in Gresham, Oregon, for dinner. As they left, I'd hugged Dad hard and said, "I love you. Now be sure and take care of yourself."

As I stood with my brothers outside, my mind was inside the house with Mother. She had been in the boat with my father and had watched him drown. As soon as I could move away from the boys I walked into the house. The words "Jean is here" moved ahead of me. Gary and I were the last ones to arrive. I slowly made my way to the dining room where Mom was waiting, stopping along the way to hug and cry with uncles, aunts, cousins, nieces, and nephews. There were about thirty family members gathered together that night.

Finally, I folded my mother into my arms, holding her as she cried, and whispered loving words into her ear. She was sixty-six years old and I was afraid she might have a heart attack from all the stress. Sobbing, she started to talk, the words spewing from her. "We were fishing, just south of the island on Detroit Lake. The fishing line became tangled around the propeller and your dad lifted the motor to try to get the line loose. He asked me to go to the front of the boat, as my weight would lift the motor higher. I turned around just in time to see the motor drop down, throwing him into the lake."

"Mom, you don't have to talk right now," I said.

"I have to tell you, I have to," she took in big gulps of air.

"OK. OK," I said softly, my own tears mingling with hers. There was absolute silence in the rest of the house.

"He surfaced. I held the oar out to him, but he was too far away to reach it. The wind was drifting the boat away from him. I threw him a life ring, but it didn't reach. He said calmly, 'Start the motor.' I started it and headed over to him, but it quit. I started it again and it stopped immediately. The wind drifted me away and I can't swim, so I couldn't help him. I just had to watch him go down. I had my shoes and socks off to jump in to be with him, but I realized if I did, no one would ever know what happened."

Taking another deep breath, her body racked with sobs, she continued. "I took the oars and paddled to the shore of the lake, then I scrambled out of the boat and tied it to the bank. I walked and ran about a mile until I finally found a cabin where a lady had a phone and she called the police for me."

I knew the rest. The sheriff located the boat and the life ring, but not my father.

I STAYED WITH MOM for the next thirteen days, while Gary remained at home with our two children. The morning after my father's death, I looked into the mirror in Mom and Dad's bathroom, and didn't recognize the person looking back at me—as if there was a part of me missing. The person in the mirror seemed out of focus, blurred, like I was moving in a fog. For the rest of the day, every time I thought of Dad I had dry heaves.

For two weeks Bob and Fred and other family members and friends searched for Dad's body, but they were unable to find him.

On May 25, we held a memorial service to celebrate his life. I wrote a "Tribute to Our Father" to be read at the service. I sobbed, screamed, and howled as I wrote, sending my anger and grief into the air. There were so many people at the service they had to set up a speaker in the entryway of the mortuary. I couldn't bear to sit in the 'family section'—it was too closed off and isolated—so the immediate family sat in the first few pews. Dad's picture stood on a table in the front and flowers were everywhere. The minister from our Episcopalian church in Gresham led the service, and my heart warmed when I heard his familiar voice read the tribute I had written. Mother appeared to be in a trance as my brothers and I surrounded her with our families.

At the end of the month, I returned home to tend to my own family and to go back to work. One of the hardest things I have ever done in my life was to leave my mother standing there as we pulled out of the driveway. My aunt Eunice, who lived two houses away, was with her, as Gary, myself and our two children drove away. Eunice had married Mother's brother Bob, who'd died in his sleep of heart failure nine months earlier. The two women had their arms around each other and waved as we left, tears spilling down their checks. They both looked small and fragile.

My parents had been married forty-nine years when Dad died, so for Mother it was like having an arm or leg amputated. She was numb for months, and didn't function well. She couldn't make decisions, so I would make suggestions on what she should do about various issues. When the bill from the mortuary came, it only showed a total charge. I asked if she would be able to call and request an itemized statement, which she did. She had to do the tasks she always did around the house and yard, and now all the things Dad had done.

A grief counselor provided some support for her, but she had nightmares that Dad was lying at the waters edge unseen. Bob arranged for a Boy Scout troop to look around the lake one weekend. We also checked into having a helicopter fly around the lake edge, but it wasn't feasible. We could have managed the cost, but they couldn't get the helicopter close enough to the shore to do a thorough search. We were able to get a death certificate, as Mother was a witness to his death and the sheriff's department determined that it was accidental. But for the next couple of years, my mother more or less just held herself together.

I WAS WATCHING TV two days after Christmas in 1985 when the phone rang. Mother's voice sounded excited, but she was crying at the same time as she told me the news. "Jean, the police just came by the house and told me that your Dad's body has been recovered from the lake."

I could hardly follow what she was saying and was afraid it wasn't true. It's probably someone else's body, I thought. After we hung up, I called Bob. He confirmed what Mother had said; the police had talked with him, also. IT WAS TRUE.

Detroit Lake is known for keeping bodies, but a miracle had occurred. After two years, seven months, and ten days, Dad's body had been found floating in the lake about a mile from where he went under. When he drowned, he had sunk into the deep cold water and hung there until the releasing body gases slowly raised him to the surface. That fall the water level in the lake was one of the lowest on record.

Because of the cold water, there were only about ten days of deterioration to his body. We didn't have to identify him, as his wallet and identification were in his pants pocket. But it wasn't until the sheriff returned Dad's wallet and glasses that I truly believed he had come home to us, to rest in the cemetery plot he'd owned for forty years.

On December 30, 1985, his two sons, son-in-law, and grandsons struggled to carry his steel gray casket from the hearse up the hill. Holding hands, Mother and I waited at the open gravesite watching the procession move toward us. This was a small group of family and close friends, nothing like the memorial service when two hundred people had attended.

Colorful poinsettias and small, decorated fir trees adorned many graves around us. The casket garland was made of the red roses he loved. The cemetery grass was brown from the dry weather we had experienced that year. The sun was shining, and although it was cold, most people were bare headed.

As the family gathered around the casket, the minister from Mother's church led us in prayer, giving thanks that John had been found and was being laid to rest beside his parents. My brothers and I stood together, beaming, feeling each other's joy at having Dad home with us. Our tears didn't fall that day.

Mother stood taller and straighter than she had for the last two and a half years, her face relaxed and peaceful. She smiled continuously and her laughter was light and came often.

After Dad was buried, we were all able to move on with our lives, but none of us were the same as we had been before his death. I thought about the way families of MIAs must feel. They would never know what happened to their loved one, and may never get a body back. Their grief process could go on forever. We had been unable to heal completely while Dad was missing, even though we knew he was in the lake.

To give some value to Dad's death and the years of grief we had experienced, I looked for a way to share what I had learned. I took a Hospice course offered at Mt. Hood College and served as a bereavement volunteer for five years, helping people through their first year of grief. For the next six years, I acted as a bereavement resource in our Peer Support Group at work. I continue to support friends and family dealing with the loss of a loved one.

Although my father has been gone for twenty-two years, and the wound from his death has healed, I still miss him.

Confessions of a Born Again

Lani Jo Leigh

IT'S FRIDAY NIGHT. I'm sitting on the top bunk singing *The Old Rugged Cross*. I love that hymn, especially the part in the chorus where you get to sing up high. My younger sister, Kathy, is asleep or she's being quiet and not talking for once. We don't call her Chatty Kathy for nothing. Mommy and Daddy are playing cards with Bernie and Lilly Fowler in the kitchen. I keep hoping they hear me. I can't sing too loud because that would seem prideful, but if I can get them to listen just a little, maybe they'll know how good I really am, and that I'm ready to get born again. Once I'm born again then maybe they'll let me go off and be a missionary in China—just like Lottie Moon.

We go to church at Shields Boulevard Baptist. We've been going there for two years—ever since I turned six. That's where we met the Fowlers and most of our friends. Going to church is almost as good as going to the circus. I've never actually been to the circus, but I remember reading about it in a first grade book, *Curious George Goes to the Circus*.

At the circus, my Sunday school teacher, Mrs. Stevens, could be the bearded lady or maybe the super, super fat lady or maybe a Siamese twin—any one of those sad, awful freaks that people gawk at in the sideshow. But she isn't fat, and she doesn't have two heads, and she doesn't have a beard. Mrs. Stevens is covered in huge, red, welty spots, each one of the spots are at least the size of a quarter, and they cover all parts of her body visible to the world—her face and her scalp poking up from underneath her hair, her arms, her hands, her legs, her feet. Maybe they're even on parts of her not visible to the world, but that's too yucky to even think about.

At first I had a sick feeling in the pit of my stomach any time I was around her. I was afraid she might hug me and I might actually have to touch one. I thought it would be like touching one of the lepers I'd heard about in the Bible. I remembered that no one could ever, ever touch a leper without becoming one, too. I was embarrassed for her, and I didn't want to look at the spots, but I guess we all have a little of Curious George in us, so I didn't want to do anything but stare at the spots. It's strange, but even with her ugly spots, Mrs. Stevens is the only person I know who seems to like herself come rain or come shine. In fact, she is so perfectly comfortable with her spots, that she makes everyone else comfortable with them, too. I don't even notice them any more; I think they must be some of God's beauty marks. Grandma always says, "God's ways are not our ways, you know." So in no time at all I love going to Mrs. Steven's Sunday school class, and every week I listen for her honey-coated laugh.

We also have a giant named Mr. Jenkins who attends church sometimes. Bernie Fowler, Jr. says he's in a kind of traveling show, so he can't come every Sunday, but when he does, he's an amazing sight to see—at least ten feet tall, give or take an inch. After church when all the other adults are standing around yapping and drinking coffee, Mr. Jenkins picks us up and throws us in the air over his head, and we're all screaming and trying to keep our dresses down over our panties, and once, my sister Carla even puked.

We've got plenty of clowns in church, too. That's what I call the church ladies (but never out loud, I don't want Daddy to tan my hide). I like the church ladies my mom's age, but the older ones whose kids are all grown up wear white gloves and huge fluffy hats with feathers and veils, and it's easy to imagine them being able to squirt water out of the enormous flower brooches on their shoulders. They wear so much pancake makeup their cheeks are an extra inch thick. I hate having to kiss the clowns, because they stink to high heaven. Mommy says it's Shalimar, but to me it's nothing but a disgusting old lady smell. I pray to God that if I should ever live to be so old as forty or fifty, I won't smell that way.

The choir sounds like trained seals. *Aarff, aarff, aarff.* I think it's because it's made up of church ladies and they warble like Jeannette MacDonald. Once I put my hands over my ears during the anthem, but Mommy gave me that evil-eye look, and then I got a spanking after church for being disrespectful.

Pastor Hart is, of course, the ringmaster. He keeps the whole show running smoothly. The pulpit is in the front on a podium set off to the right side of the church, and he towers over us. With thick gray hair and a deep, booming voice, he stands for God, he is God, cracking the whip, and barking, "Trust in Jesus. Come to Jesus or face the fires of hell." He'll scare anyone out of going to hell.

HELL IS THE FIERY HOME of the devil and his angels, and I know I'm bound for there if I don't get born again. I don't worry about monsters under my bed; I know there's no such thing as monsters. But the devil's demons live under the beds of all bad boys and girls, and they're always waiting and watching to grab our legs and pull us under and take us down to hell where we'll be tormented day and night. Tormenting is something my little sister does to me with her constant yapping and running around in circles. My mom is for ever saying, "Kathy Ann, stop tormentin' your sister." I can't imagine anything worse than an eternity of being tormented by my sister, burning in fire, and no Jesus.

Jesus lives in heaven and if I want to live with Jesus, I need to get born again. When that happens I'll be washed in the blood of the lamb. I will be a new person, the best person I can possibly be, and I want it so desperately. That's why I'm singing up here on the bed. Maybe Mommy and Daddy will hear me and know I'm ready. And then I can get baptized, and never have to worry about anything ever again. Unless I grow up and become a backslider (like my Uncle Ronald, heaven forbid), but I love Jesus so much, I don't see how that could happen.

IT'S SUNDAY NIGHT. I'm sitting in church, fifth row from the front. Our family takes up the whole row. My dad sits next to the outside aisle. Next to him is Mommy, and she's holding my baby brother in her arms. Then it's us four girls. Jan is next to Mommy. I'm between her and Carla. Kathy is on the end. I've been listening closely to everything Pastor Hart's been saying. I think I hear Jesus talking to me, so maybe tonight is the night. Pastor Hart has come down from the pulpit. He's standing at the front of the center aisle and the church deacons are in the front pew, watching and waiting to see if anyone wants to get saved. This is an altar call—my altar call. We're singing "Just as I am without one plea, but that Thy blood was shed for me. And that Thou bidst me come to Thee, O Lamb of God, I come, I come."

Yes, they're singing for me. Jesus wants me to come on down to the front, kneel with the deacon, and ask Him into my heart. That's the only way to do it—the only way I can get born again.

I crawl over my little sisters and make my way out to the aisle. I look over at Mommy. Why is she crying? Everyone is still singing, but I can't make out all the words—there's a roaring in my ears and I think my heart is bursting inside my chest. I don't have far to go, but this walk down the aisle feels like it's taking hours. Deacon Tyler is coming up to me. I whisper that I want to be born again. He can't hear me over my heartbeat; I've got to speak up louder: *Deacon Tyler, I want to be born again.*

"All right, child. repeat after me. I want Jesus"

I want Jesus

"To be my Lord and Savior."

To be my Lord and Savior.

"Amen."

Amen.

That's it? I'm born again? Are you sure? I don't feel different. I'm supposed to be as white as snow. Why do I still worry about the devil? What is it that Pastor Hart says, "God said it, I believe it, and that's the end of it?" I don't know—I just have to trust in God, I guess. At least now I can get baptized and maybe then I'll stop fearing hell and the devil's wrath.

THE BAPTISMAL FONT is at the front of the church—like a fish tank the size of our pickup truck. Usually a heavy red curtain covers the font and the choir sits in front of it. But after the church service, when it's time for a baptism, the choir sits in the pews with the rest of the congregation, and the curtain is pulled to each side just like we're at the movie theater. There is a small dressing room on each side of the font—men on the right, women on the left. I go to the left side and wait my turn. One of the church ladies helps me put on a white robe. She says I can keep my underwear on, and my mom made sure I had clean panties and an undershirt. I don't have titties yet, but I do have little nipples, and I wouldn't want anyone to see them.

My baptismal robe is whiter than my dad's Sunday dress shirts. It's like the piercing white of a lightning strike on a humid July night. Mrs. Clark hugs me, whispers, "Jesus loves you," and the robe takes on the smell of Shalimar. As I climb the half dozen steps down into the water I feel like I'm choking. I want to look for my sisters and wave to them from the top step, but I know I'm not supposed to act like that any more. The water is so warm it makes me want to pee, just like in summer when we're swimming down at Sulphur Springs. The water is deep, and I'm afraid my feet won't touch the bottom. I can see my little bare feet dangling under the robe while I clutch at Pastor Hart's arm. Dear God, please don't let me drown, and please, please don't let me pee.

Pastor places one huge hand the size of a first base mitt tightly under my neck, and the other hand completely covers my nose and mouth. In a booming voice he says, "Lani Jo, I baptize you in the name of the Father." Then he pulls down with the hand under my neck and pushes down with the hand covering my face until I am under the water. He pulls me up sputtering, and then pushes me down into the water again. "And of the Son." He quickly draws me back up through the water only to push me down again for the third and final time. "And of the Holy Ghost." Thank God there's only three of Him 'cause I can't hold my breath much longer.

Finally Pastor Hart brings me back up out of the water, and he guides me to the steps leading to the dressing room. I can hardly move; the heavy, wet robe is plastered to my skin and I feel like a mummy entombed forever. I get dressed, and afterwards we go out for ice cream. Mommy and Daddy tell me how proud they are of me. My Grandma gives me a new Bible with my baptismal date written in the front underneath my name. I'm not sure why, but I start crying, right in the middle of eating my black walnut ice cream cone. I think it's probably just relief that I didn't drown while I was in the font, because if I had I might still have fallen into the devil's clutches.

I PRACTICALLY GROW UP in the church; my dad's a deacon and family attendance is mandatory twice on Sunday, Wednesday night, and every night during a revival. There remain many things about God and religion that I don't understand. Like why my friend, Betty, who's a Methodist, can dance and I can't. I really, really want to dance. I want to take ballet lessons and wear those sweet pink slippers and a wonderful pink tutu. But Baptists don't dance. I also want to be a Girl Scout, but that isn't allowed either. I have to belong to Girls Auxiliary, and instead of going camping or learning how to make porcupines out of Styrofoam balls and toothpicks, I have to learn the names of every country where Southern Baptists have missionaries. And we have to perform sword drills. In a sword drill, all the children in class must close their Bibles and hold them firmly by the binder. Then the leader shouts "sheathe swords," and at this point the children put their Bibles under their arms. When the leader shouts, "draw swords," the children hold their Bibles in the air with straight arms. The leader tells the children a book, a chapter, and a verse of the Bible, for example, "John chapter three verse sixteen." Once the children have repeated the reference, the leaders shouts, "charge, " and the children try to look up the verse as quickly as possible. The first child to find the reference shouts out the first few words from the verse. Sounds like the perfect way to spend a Sunday evening. I like reading the Bible and I try to use it to my advantage. Psalm 150, verse 4, even tells us to praise God with dancing, but my parents aren't buying it.

WHEN I'M OLDER, about twelve, I'm convinced that I couldn't have really been saved at eight because I didn't at all understand what I was doing. My religion had been simple and uncomplicated—I love Jesus and Jesus loves me. Now I'm learning that it's much more complicated than that. How can an eight-year-old child know about atonement and redemption, grace and forgiveness? And how can an eight-year-old child fully appreciate the depth of her wickedness, and understand that Jesus had to suffer and die to save her from her sin? So I get born again, again. And baptized again. This time at least I can touch the bottom of the baptismal font.

By THE TIME I get into high school I am pretty sure my religion is all a load of crap. Being Baptist means a bunch of "don'ts." Don't drink, don't smoke, don't do drugs, don't dance, don't have sex, don't ask questions, don't feel happy, don't be human. I don't smoke, drink or do drugs, but I sure want to dance. And having sex sure makes me happy. My boyfriend, Randall, and I start going at it hot and heavy by the end of our sophomore year.

In early January 1971, the second semester of my junior year, I start getting really sick in the morning. *Please, please God, let it be food poisoning, let it be a stomach virus.* Randall and I had tried to be careful—pulling his cock out of me before he came, avoiding (when possible) certain days of the month—but when you're seventeen the rhythm system is far from an ideal means of birth control. I go to see Dr. Davidson, our family doctor, and on a bitter morning with a knife blade wind cutting across the plains, he calls me at home before school to tell me I'm pregnant. "And, Lani, you need to tell your parents this week, or I'll have to call them myself with the news."

Oh, my God, what am I going to do? I need to find Randall; I need to find my best friend, Darlene. I catch the bus to school, and go to my first class of the morning, French. This was my second year in French class, and one of my favorites. The previous year Mrs. Tourney took us on a field trip to a

French restaurant, and we got to eat snails. This morning, I sit in class crying, feeling so scared and all alone. Mrs. Tourney comes in, and she's been crying, too. "I have bad news to share with you. Kyla's brother, Ian, died last night. The wake is scheduled for Thursday."

I'm sure there's a lightning storm in our tiny classroom. Its astonishing force cuts through the heart of me. Ian and I had been friends for years. I think back to an end of the year party for our tenth grade honors English class. We went to the duck pond at the University of Oklahoma, had a picnic, read poetry, and acted like fifteen-year-old fools. Ian brought a bottle of cheap wine to help us all celebrate. His parents kept wine in the house, and they even let him drink it sometimes. They were Irish Catholics, and, unlike Baptists, drinking just wasn't the biggest sin in the world. At the time, I quite admired their sophisticated attitude, and wondered what it would take to become Catholic when I was older.

I can't believe Ian is dead. Everyone keeps calling it a freak accident— Ian supposedly stumbled down the stairs to his basement and got entangled in a rope—a misfortunate hanging. I don't think anyone, especially his Catholic family, wants to admit that it was suicide.

Sanctimonious Baptists have their own idea of what constitutes salvation. At church we are told that Ian was a good person, but he wasn't "saved," and that could only mean one thing for Ian—he was going to hell. We are told that this was the reason we have to redouble our evangelism efforts—bring everyone we know to Jesus—because we can't let our friends go to hell—they all must be born again. I determine then and there that I would rather go to hell and drink wine with Ian than go to heaven and be bored stiff with a bunch of holier-than-thou misers.

As for the pregnancy, I tell Randall and Darlene sometime the week of Ian's funeral. At home, I interrupt the weekly family prayer meeting and Bible Study with the news. My options are few: abortion was illegal,

Randall didn't want to marry me and keep the baby, and I am told that I am not ready or able to care for a baby on my own. My mom and dad and I meet with our pastor, and the decision is made that I leave Oklahoma, go to a Southern Baptist maternity home, and give the baby up for adoption. And after spending six months there and losing my baby for what I thought was forever, I am pretty damn sure that there can't be any God in this world.

TEN YEARS OF NO CHURCH, and no God. Ten years of believing that all I have, all I can find, is inside of me. Ten years of a spiritual wasteland. Ten years of walking alone.

AT TWENTY-SEVEN I'm divorced with two children and dead broke. One Sunday a new boyfriend takes me to an Episcopal church. I feel strange at first, this is so much like what I had heard a Catholic church would be like—there is an altar and incense, candles and icons, Holy Communion, real bread and real wine. The priest comes by with outstretched hands and whispered words, and my tears start flowing. I stay on my knees feeling like I've come in out of the cold. God has wrapped me in a blanket; and I feel enveloped by love for the first time in many, many years. My head keeps saying, "this is crazy, you've gone insane and over to the dark side." But my heart just feels loved. In the dim stillness, in the bread and the wine, in the quiet presence of the community I can see and taste God. And so I keep coming back—week after week—to be filled with grace.

I RECOGNIZE THAT MY AWARENESS and understanding of God is no greater than a butterfly's awareness and understanding of me. I consider organized religion far from perfect, yet I believe religion can be a conduit for seeking and finding God. I could easily be a Buddhist, a Hindu, a

Muslim, or a Jew. Having grown up "born again," I feel comfortable using the language of Christianity to articulate my spiritual beliefs, though there is a lot about the Christian faith that I find disagreeable. So I pick and choose. I use images and icons and words that work for me and continue to lead me to God, and I ignore the rest. Expressing my faith is no longer about the "don'ts," it's about the "do's." "Do justice, love mercy, walk humbly."

I go to church each week for community and communion and because it's the one place in this world where I can warble like Jeannette McDonald—I sing and sing until my heart's content. I feel part of something that has stood a long time—a continuous stream of truth seekers who pass from generation to generation a desire to know and be known. I've become one of the dreaded church ladies, but thankfully there are no gloves, hats, or the stink of Shalimar.

And I think that I probably had it right all along. Not the part about the devil or hell; they're just some bogeyman stories to scare little children. But in my childlike way, I understood that my spiritual life could boil down to something as simple as "I love Jesus and Jesus loves me." Especially now that I can see Jesus, not as some far off dead and resurrected historical figure, but as God's continual manifestation in our world. Jesus is me, and every person that crosses my path.

So I have to open myself up to love, because in the beginning and in the end that's all we've got to go on—God is Love.

Learning to Write

Frances Kiva

SLOWLY, THE SHRINE has been disappearing, erasing the moment of her death which had sat frozen in his apartment for almost two years. The change had moved through the living room, taking first her reading glasses and the *TV Guide* opened perpetually to July 27, 2003. Then her half glass of water stopped being refilled. The flowers finally died and were not meticulously replaced. He re-arranged the furniture to fit his tastes.

The healing passage of time had compelled him to continue to move the changes into her bedroom with a subtle touch at first—the last teddy bear she had bought me when I turned twelve was found in a box in storage and propped up in a chair next to her bed. Then some new photographs unearthed in another box were framed and set on her dresser. Finally, on the walls, went beautiful watercolors of flowers. It became the perfected room that his memory of her would love to inhabit.

When I visit my stepfather to make my own pilgrimage to her Shrine, I take note of these changes, liking how he remembers my mother. He has not yet moved his memory of her into her walk-in-closet, not yet rearranged how she left things to fit how he wants to remember her. So this is where I go to remember. I can stand among her neatly hung clothes accumulated throughout her life and she will be at my house on Christmas Eve in that green silk shirt. Or she will be holding my hand as we walk gingerly over hot sand at the beach, her feet in those leather sandals. I can run my hand over the fox stole and almost remember a woman before she was my mother, beautiful and well-dressed, turning heads on a New York city street. And there, hanging on a hook is a brown purse, its leather still as supple in my hands as it was almost thirty-five years ago, sending me back to a sunny afternoon.

I'M TRYING TO make my dirty blue Keds match her steps as we walk up our street. Her feet small in her white sandals with the square heel always are a bit a head of me, no matter how I try to stretch my legs.

"What movie are we going to see, Mommy?"

"*The Sting.*"

"Oh." I step, stretch, jump. I don't want to step on the cracks in the sidewalk. "Is it about bees?"

"No, it's about people. It has Robert Redford in it, and Paul Newman. They're both really famous actors. It might get an Academy Award."

"Oh."

I jump my way down our street, trying to land in the center of each sidewalk square. "Mommy, don't step on the cracks—you'll break your mother's back."

"OK, honey, I won't." She continues walking, altering her step to my demand as we make our way past our neighbors' houses.

"Is Mrs. Bird a witch?" There is her brown house. Its overgrown lot always made it dark inside.

"No—what makes you say that?"

"Everyone says she's a witch."

"No, she's not. Her son died in the war and she hasn't been the same since. I want you to be nice to her and not say mean things."

It was easy to be nice to her. She never came out of her house. When I went there she always gave me nice pink candies. She was too old to have a son, I thought. She looked like a grandmother. And it was fun to run past her driveway fast with my friends, our fear chasing us. I hope she didn't see us do that because I liked the sticky sweet pink candies.

"Hello, Mrs. Bates." A voice stops my mother in front of me. The voice belongs to a man doing something in his yard.

My mother pauses, looking at the long-haired, bearded man making his way over to us. "John? Is that you?"

He laughs and shakes his hair out of his face. "Yeah, it's me, Mrs. Bates. My parents have been after me to cut it."

"Oh, no, it's fine. I just didn't know you were back. Your parents must be so glad."

"Yeah, well, after the war—I've been…uh, traveling around a bit."

"Oh, how was that?"

Looking down I notice an ant hill. They are trying to carry a large seed into their hole. It doesn't fit. They keep passing the seed between them, trying other approaches. They are small men building a great city underground. They need my help. I pick the seed off their backs and push it down the hole. They all cheer, thanking me. The city will be named Frances the Great.

"…well it certainly is quite a belt buckle." My mother is laughing.

"It does get some comments," he laughs back.

I look at the belt buckle. It has letters on it. I know those letters. I almost know all my letters. I pick up a stick near the ant hill and begin to draw in the dirt as they keep talking. I glance back at the belt-buckle that made my mother laugh. The first letter is easy. It is the same letter as my name. I copy it into the dirt.

F

I can't remember the next letter without looking. Oh wait, I know—

U

The next letter is in my name too, but toward the end. I copy it in the dirt next to the other two.

C

The last letter I have to look at two times to get right. I write it backward first, then, crossing it out I write it correctly.

K

I write it in the dirt with the stick, practicing my letters until I'm hot and bored. I stand up and lean my head against my mother, her purse against my cheek, its warm leather scent in my nose. Closing my eyes I trace the word with my finger against the soft leather—over and over as she talked and talked.

"OK, Frannie, let's go or we'll miss our movie." Finally, her voice jerked my head up. In front of me is her brown purse with the belt-buckle word scratched in the leather. It will come out, I think. My mother is good at cleaning things. I follow her up the street.

I'm SWINGING, flying to the sky, touching the top of the trees that frame my back yard.

"FRANCES! COME HERE RIGHT NOW!"

Cringing, I force myself to run into the house. I know that tone. My mind races to remember what I could have done wrong.

As soon as I enter the kitchen I know. All I can see is the leather purse in her hand.

"WHY DID YOU DO THIS?"

I look at my feet for an answer. They don't say anything. "I don't know." I mumble.

"Well I DO! You were mad at me for making you wait the other day. Why else would you have done this?" She waves the purse so close to my face I have to move not to be hit with it. "Do you have any idea how much this cost? And…I, I had to walk around with this word ALL day where everyone could see it. I can't believe you would do this, and with such an awful word, too!" She's holding the purse the way I've seen her hold the dead mice the cat brings in.

The tears start making their way out of my eyes. It's an awful word? One of those words that you are not supposed to say. "I didn't know Mommy. I thought you liked the word on his belt buckle."

"Why would I like this word? And most of all—why would I want it on my purse?" She is shaking her head at me, eyebrows puckered in disbelief, her thin lips sucked in. Finally, she lets out a breath. "Why are you always so bad?"

"I'm so sorry, Mommy. I didn't mean to hurt your purse. I thought it would come out. Please don't be mad."

She looks down at me for a minute, quietly. "Sit down." I sit. I hear her rummaging in a drawer behind me. She pulls out a notebook and pen. "Here." She puts them in front of me. "When I was little if we got in trouble we had to write lines saying 'I will not do…' whatever it was. I want you to write out 'I will not use the word fuck' one hundred times." She writes the sentence across the top of my paper for me to copy.

A hundred times later my hand is cramped and the word fuck indelibly imprinted on my mind. It later becomes one of my most used "awful" words.

I KNEW SHE had kept this purse all these years hanging in the back of her closet, one side carefully turned to the wall. I used to look at it and think she kept it because she couldn't bear to get rid of an expensive purse, no matter how ruined. Sometimes she would take it out, a small scolding smile hanging around her mouth, and say "Do you remember when you did this?" I would cringe at the painful memory of being punished, and how I was inadvertently "bad."

Today, as I turn over the purse in my hands, a mother myself, and I see my childish scrawl in the leather, finally I know why she kept it all these years. It isn't a memory of being bad, but a loving memento of a little child and a young mother learning together. I trace my finger over the "awful" word on the soft leather and I like the new memory of my mother keeping the purse all these years. Gently, I hang it back on the hook, careful to make sure I have the unmarred side out, just as she would have liked it. Quietly, I leave the Shrine, taking this memory with me.

Contributors

Adrian Shirk goes to high school part time, but is mostly a free bird. She works for a non-profit organization, selling used clothing online. She plays tambourine in a jug-music band, and wrote her teenage memoir, *Walking in the Streets was Less Dangerous.*

Amanda Risser is a family practice doctor in Portland. She recently finished her residency and is just starting to recover. What got her through it? Her dear partner Eli, her community of co-residents and friends, at least one scotch nightly (when not on call), delivering babies, and caring for an endless variety of people who tell her their stories.

Amy Lee is not a symbol. She's just a girl who thinks she's a boy.

Ann Rogers-Williams is a writer, printmaker, personal historian, and mother of two teenagers. Her passion is helping older adults recognize and develop their own creative potential through legacy arts. She is earning a certificate in Gerontology and has recently completed training in creativity coaching.

Ariel Gore teaches the Memoir Workshop at The Attic. She's the author of five books including *The Traveling Death and Resurrection Show*, upcoming from HarperSanFrancisco in 2006. Click to www.arielgore.com.

Emily A. Phillips comes from Strasburg, Virginia. She moved to the west coast with her cat Stevie Wonder in 2001 and has been a secret poet since she was ten.

Fontaine Roberson lives with her husband and two daughters in Portland. Her premature baby is now a healthy four-year-old, and a great big sister.

Frances Kiva, a political refugee from Southern California, has really nice teeth.

Geraldo Valerio is a writer and illustrator who recently fled the insanity to Canada. His work has appeared in publications including *Spork* and *Hip Mama*.

Helena Carlson grew up in Dublin in the hard old times. She lived in a family with a Protestant father and a Catholic mother. They also had a Jewish branch of the family. Politics were rarely discussed.

Hope C. Hitchcock is a wicked nanny.

Jean Braden is a grandmother and didn't start writing until she retired. She lives in Gresham, Oregon, and is writing a story detailing her family's move from Nebraska to Oregon in 1934.

Jessica Byers was born in London, grew up in Cambridge, Massachusetts, and began keeping a journal at age seven. She now resides in North Portland with the sweetest cat in the world and works as a concert promoter. See www.shiningcitymusic.com.

Kelli Grinich lives with her husband and three children in McMinnville, Oregon. She charts the clouds as they move over the coast range while she contemplates what to write next.

Krystee Sidwell is a cowgirl-turned-karaoke-star.

Lainie Keslin Ettinger is a freelance writer. She lives in Portland with her husband and two daughters.

Lani Jo Leigh is a wild sexy complicated grandmother of two. Raised in Oklahoma, she now lives in Portland with her husband of seventeen years. She is finishing a novel, *Prodigal Mom*, based on her experiences as an unwed teenager forced to live in a maternity home and give her baby up for adoption in 1971. A filmmaker, she makes documentaries when serious and porn for fun.

Linda Fielder works at the humane society. She does not want to adopt your misbehaved dog.

Linda Hefferman's writing career came to a halt in the fourth grade when she misunderstood the details of baby-making. She shelved the novel she was writing at the time and decided to grow up instead. The facts of life now fully in hand, she's writing a travelogue/memoir about giving birth in Paris.

Lori Maliszewski spent over twenty years working in high-tech marketing, all the while searching for the perfect cup of coffee.

Margaret McConnell is a west coast writer whose work has appeared in the anthology *A Woman Alone: Travel Tales from Around the Globe*, and in publications including *Hip Mama* and *Nervy Girl*. She is currently living and writing in Andhra Pradesh, India. Can you be a west coast writer living in Andhra Pradesh?

Maria Fabulosa is commie acupuncturist and musician on sabbatical. She's typing her novel, *The Ghost of Zucamuya*, on an old Smith Corona.

Mary Jane Kelly was named Mary Jane after her dad's P-38, a name synonymous with guts and hard luck in his family. He loved his little sister for it, so she's guessing he loved her the same.

Mira Shah is a pediatric speech pathologist in Portland. Her formative years were spent navigating the southern states of Kentucky and Georgia in a bi-cultural family with ties to neither state. She has no plans to marry—even if same-sex marriage becomes as commonplace as corduroy pants.

Rachael Duke won the Worthington, Ohio library poetry contest in fifth grade and also has a short story which appears (under the name Rachael Silverman) in *The Spirit of Pregnancy*. She really likes to show up at her kids' classrooms and play music so that everyone can sing together. Her oldest son has informed her that this will have to stop by middle school.

Rachel Indigo Cerise Baum's stark, staccato, brutally honest writing, zines, lyrics, and art can be found at http://ricerisebaum.livejournal.com.

Printed in the United States
46573LVS00009B/64

9 781411 663053